all russians love birch trees

all russians
love
birch trees

OLGA GRJASNOWA

Translated from the German by Eva Bacon

OTHER PRESS
NEW YORK

Originally published in German as *Der Russe ist einer, der Birken liebt* by Carl Hanser Verlag, Munich, in 2012.

Translation copyright © Eva Bacon, 2014

The translation of this work was supported by a grant from the Goethe-Institut that is funded by the German Ministry of Foreign Affairs.

Chekhov epigraph from *The Complete Plays,* translated by Laurence Senelick (New York: Norton, 2006).

Production Editor: Yvonne E. Cárdenas
Text Designer: Jennifer Daddio/Bookmark Design & Media, Inc.
This book was set in 12 pt Simoncini Garamond by
Alpha Design & Composition of Pittsfield, NH.

1 3 5 7 9 10 8 6 4 2

Library of Congress Cataloging-in-Publication Data

Grjasnowa, Olga, 1984- author.
[Russe ist einer, der Birken liebt. English]
All Russians love birch trees / by Olga Grjasnowa ; [translation by Eva Bacon].
pages cm
ISBN 978-1-59051-584-6 (pbk.) — ISBN 978-1-59051-585-3 (ebook)
1. Jews—Azerbaijan—Fiction. 2. Jews, Russian—Germany—Fiction. 3. Jews, Russians—Israel—Fiction. 4. Jewish women—Fiction. I. Bacon, Eva, translator. II. Title.
PT2707.R587R8713 2014
833'.92—dc23
2013008395

Publisher's Note:
This is a work of fiction. Names, characters, places, and incidents either are the product of the author's imagination or are used fictitiously, and any resemblance to actual persons, living or dead, events, or locales is entirely coincidental.

Vershinin: Why should you care? Here there's such a wholesome, bracing Russian climate. A forest, a river . . . and birch trees here too. Dear, humble birches, I love them more than any other tree. It's a good place to live. Only it's odd, the train station is over thirteen miles away . . . And nobody knows why that is.

Anton Chekhov
Three Sisters

part one

1

I didn't want this day to begin. I would rather have stayed in bed and kept sleeping, but the laughter of the fruit vendor and the rattle of the streetcar invaded our bedroom through the wide-open window. Our apartment wasn't far from the central station, which basically meant that in our neighborhood there were streets better left avoided, with discount stores and huge erotic cinemas. Here—between an old Chinese Laundromat and a left-leaning youth center, whose visitors often mistook our front door for a urinal—was our home. Our apartment was ramshackle and rundown, but cheap. Every morning at about five o'clock, fathers, brothers, and cousins unloaded their vans beneath our windows.

They slammed their doors and assembled their stands, drank tea, roasted corn on the cob, and waited. They waited for the street to fill so that they could advertise their fruit in automated singsong voices. I tried to follow their conversations, but mostly just understood a bit here and there, or fell asleep again.

Elias was lying next to me: stirring, lips slightly parted, eyelids fluttering, irregular rise and fall of his chest. "Fucking pig faggot, I'll kill you!" yelled a drunk under our window. The fruit vendors laughed at him and spit sunflower shells onto the street.

Elias woke up and turned toward me. Without opening his eyes, he rested his head on my stomach. His hands followed mine. We stayed there, wedged together, until someone else's alarm clock went off behind the wall and my hand grew numb beneath his weight. When it went completely numb I climbed out of bed to take a shower.

The kitchen was crammed with yesterday's dishes. Pots and pans with crusty rims, plates and half-full wineglasses were stacked on top of each other on the counter. The air smelled like exhaust and stuck to my skin like syrup. It was going to be the hottest day of the year.

Elias was sitting at the kitchen table. In his right hand was a spoon full of granola. Crumbs were scattered in front of him. Half a roll sat on a plate, covered in a dark red layer of jam. I took a seat facing him, reached for the newspaper, and then, instead of the paper, studied his face. He had high cheekbones, gray-blue eyes, and dark lashes just a little on the short side. Elias was little-boy-pretty. His good looks annoyed him—people would never remember him as a person, but as someone resembling an actor, whose name they never quite remembered. It wasn't his beauty, but rather his intuitive politeness that gave him the effect he had—on impatient cash register ladies, who suddenly forgot to check their watches, on giggling schoolgirls, medical assistants, librarians, and me. First and foremost on me. The gifts of a con man, my mother said. But she loved him, because of those gifts especially, and because Elias, for whatever reason, knew how to behave around an Eastern family.

He poured coffee into his granola. White dissolving into brown and raisins bobbing on the surface. On the kitchen table, under the newspaper, lay an open cookbook. On the page a fish's head stared out at me questioningly. I flipped it shut.

"I hate to remind you, you're a vegetarian!" I said jokingly.

"At least I check what it is that I'm putting into the oven," he replied, irritated.

He was alluding to the night before. I had attempted to make a quiche because I wanted to try out the word *quiche* for my vocabulary. As if I were a French actress playing a French housewife awaiting her French lover, who was returning from the war an invalid, and she is baking a quiche for him, not knowing which limb he's lost. *Quiche* rolled nicely off my tongue. *La quiche.* I'd purchased frozen shortcrust pastry, which turned out to be sweet shortcrust pastry. The quiche was inedible.

In France the dough was neither sweet nor salty. Elias ate my quiche anyway. I hadn't insisted on this polite gesture, but he was still suffering from the after-effects of his good education. He had immediately washed down every bite with water.

"Have you seen my shin pads?" Elias asked as I was rifling through the fridge, searching for the quiche.

"Have you seen dinner?" I asked.

"I put it in the freezer."

"What?"

"I didn't think you still wanted it."

"You always have to play the compassionate German, huh?" I asked. Elias grinned, pushing the milk and the granola toward me and getting me a bowl from the shelf. I took a seat and sorted my school stuff into one neat pile—notepads, vocabulary lists, flash cards, and dictionaries that I memorized from *A* to *Z*. When Elias returned to the table, he softly kissed the top of my head and asked again: "Have you seen my shin pads?"

"I already told you."

"But you always lose things."

"No idea where they are," I said.

He carefully put the dishes into the sink, making sure that the plates didn't touch each other.

"And since when do you play soccer?" I asked. "And with whom?"

"I've played before."

"I'm sure you'll break something."

"Do I need an *immigrant background* to play soccer?" he asked, looking me straight in the eye.

"Not that again." I tried to sound as ironic as possible, but without much success. Whenever I came across this expression I could feel bile rising in my throat. The only thing worse was the adjective *postmigrant*. I hated the discussions related to these words, not only the public ones, but also the ones between the two of us. Nothing new was ever said in these conversations, but the tone was patronizing and strident. One of us provoked disagreement and then we both got caught up in allegations and rebukes. Elias accused me of caginess and I blamed him for being pushy, at which point he tended to move from general to specific claims.

Elias looked offended, so I went over to him and he placed his hands on my hips. On his chin hung a single dark-blond hair. I removed it. He rested his head on my shoulder, I kissed his neck and pushed my knee between his legs and unbuttoned my summer dress a little. But Elias shook his head and whispered: "I'm running late."

I slammed my palm onto the counter. Elias shot me an accusing glance and said: "I didn't mean it like that."

"My grandma once said always have a pair of fresh panties on you."

"Why?"

"In case something happens."

"You're crazy. And I have to go."

I accompanied Elias to the door and watched him run down the stairs. He always took two steps at once, sometimes three. He never walked, he leaped and ran. I made myself a coffee and started studying.

2

The information desk was manned by a nurse who was wearing a long pullover, despite the heat. She was pale, which accentuated her flaming red hair, pulled tightly into a bun. She smiled sweet-and-sourly and told me not to worry needlessly and to refrain from further inquiries. I had run all the way to the hospital and was now standing in front of her, drenched in sweat, red-faced and completely out of breath. Elias was in surgery.

I sat down in the waiting room. A radio was on in the background. I translated the news simultaneously into English, the ads into French. In Kabul there had been an explosion, in Gaza shots were fired, and in Portugal the forests were burning. The chancellor was on a state visit. I flipped through an old issue of *Vogue* and waited in fashion. Handbags. Jewelry. Eye shadow. Whatever. I read about last November's trends: fur and floral prints. I tore out the first page, folded it, and put it into my bag. Then I tore page three out, folded it, and put it into my bag. Page five got torn out as well, folded and put into my bag. By page 107 my bag was full.

A doctor approached, smiling. He was tall and broad-shouldered. Hair brushed back neatly. As a greeting he folded my hand into his and held it just a bit too long. His eyes were brown and very alert. The smell of disinfectant, decay, and old people engulfed me. I gasped for air. The doctor put his hand on my arm and I was surprised by the intrusiveness of the gesture. He said something, but I didn't hear him and had to ask again.

"Do you speak German?" he asked slowly, over-enunciating each word.

"Of course," I answered.

"My name is Weiss. Resident Physician Weiss. Are you a family member of Elias Angermann?"

"I'm his girlfriend."

"Then I guess I'm not really supposed to speak with you."

"That shouldn't be a problem, should it?"

He reflected for a moment. The decision seemed not to come easily. Finally he nodded and said, "Oh well. What is your name?"

"Maria Kogan."

He regarded me from head to toe. "I'm not sure I would pronounce your last name correctly. Can I call you Maria?"

"No."

He shrugged. His voice growing louder with each syllable, he explained that a nail had been inserted into Elias's femur. An intramedullary fixation. That they had nailed metal plates to the thighbone and that Elias had lost a lot of blood. I noticed splatters of blood on his lab coat and wondered whether they had come from Elias or a patient before. I nodded and opened the door of the anesthetic recovery room. The recovery would be a long one, the doctor's voice reverberated behind me. The room was empty, save a bed that was fenced in by monitors, tubes, and a single chair. The curtains were closed. I opened them just a little, so that a sliver of light sliced across the floor. I lay my hand on the bedrails. Elias's face was wan, as if every last drop of blood had drained from his body. A thin white crust caked his lips. He murmured my name and looked past me. A surgical drain emerged from his thigh.

I bent down and the smell of cold sweat reached my nose. I kissed his forehead and stroked his hair. He moaned. I extended my hand to touch his, but then I saw the IV drip in the back of his hand, hesitated, and withdrew.

"I'm not doing so well," Elias said so quietly that he couldn't possibly have meant for me to hear it, and suddenly a memory came back to mind, of him remarking that there are only two schools: old school and the Frankfurt School.

I stayed until late. Feverish Elias hoisted his head from side to side. At times an "Are you still there?" punctured his restless sleep.

That evening I made myself an instant soup and called his parents. Nobody picked up. I thought about calling Elke on her cellphone, but I already heard myself leaving a voicemail. "Hi, it's Masha. Hey." I paused and bit my lip. "Elias slipped while playing soccer. He broke his thighbone. He's in the hospital." The sentences came out labored. It had been a decade since I'd struggled so much to speak German. Elke called back in the middle of the night. Was it bad? No, I assured her. She said she couldn't leave the restaurant. Every night it's busy. I told her that I'm here. Elke said she'd try to come as soon as possible. I told her not to worry, I'm here.

I packed a bag for Elias. I folded his underwear, T-shirts, and the sole pair of pajamas in his possession. Then I added his overnight bag, his camera, a sketchbook, and charcoal pencils.

His roommates were watching afternoon talk shows. TV sounds blended in with snippets of conversation and laughter, the rustling of candy wrappers and magazines, the squeaking of shoes, and the wheels of food trolleys in the hallway.

Elias was lying in the middle, his bed flanked by two other beds. Beside every bed was a little nightstand. His neighbors' tables were piled high with chocolate bars, open packs of cookies, bags of gummi bears, Sudoku books, cigarettes, and magazines. I said hello to everyone in the room, but nobody paid attention to me.

Elias lay pale and dull-eyed in his hospital bed. I put on a smile and approached him. I sat the bag down next to his table and listed out what I had brought. Like Christmas, Elias joked, exhausted.

Elias spent most of the time sleeping, dazed by medication. Only breathing in and out. I sat next to his bed, peeled sour apples, pears, and a mango. The mango juice stuck to my fingers. I drank coffee and disappeared into the bathroom, where I splashed cold water onto my face to fend off tears and a headache. The morning and the afternoon passed. The sun set excruciatingly slowly. Outside the shadows got longer and Elias's hand rested in mine.

By the next morning, he was already taking photos of the room, of his wound, and of me, who wasn't able to look at his wound. The roommates also wanted to get some camera time. They were done playing cards and now forced us into conversation. He wouldn't want to miss out on the opportunity to get his picture taken by a professional, Heinz said, when he learned that Elias studied photography.

Heinz had served in World War II and Rainer was a locksmith. There were some things they would do differently today. Though not much, of course, not much. The person in the bed to the left of Elias cleared his throat and said he had to pay me a compliment. That my German is better than that of any Russian Germans he's met at the social services office. I had hardly said anything yet. Heinz started talking about his time as a prisoner of war—until Elias asked him to please be quiet. Then Elias asked me to be quiet as well.

It was hot and humid. The asphalt reflected the heat and even at night the streets didn't cool. I got off my bike in front of the hospital and wiped the sweat off my forehead. The bicycle rack was filled to capacity, so I pushed my bike a bit. Then I spotted a free rack after all and squeezed it in. The green bike on the left fell and I laboriously brought it back to an upright position.

The hospital was an elongated low-rise with a stone facade that stood in the middle of a residential area—an edifice completely devoid of architectural ambition and solely intended to best serve its medical purpose. The resident physician who had removed Elias's surgical drain the day before sat in front of the entrance to the orthopedic ward and smoked. He had dark circles under his eyes and unkempt hair. I had seen him yesterday afternoon in the hospital and he looked as if he had worked through the night. He nodded toward me and I slowed until I waveringly stopped right in front of him. He held out his cigarette pack, light blue with Arabic letters. I offered him a croissant. He breathed out smoke and reached into my bag. The skin of his hand was cragged, his nails had yellowed from the tobacco.

"Did you switch to filtered cigarettes recently?"

"Not really. Those are from a patient." He looked down at the pack, turning it over a couple of times and running his thumb over the Arabic letters as if he'd just noticed them for the first time.

"I can't read it," he said.

I translated the text for him.

He sighed, never taking his eyes off the pack.

"The patient died yesterday afternoon. We're finishing off his last cigarettes."

I choked on the smoke and had to cough.

He turned the pack over a couple of times more, then put it back into his pocket. He took a bite of the croissant, crumbs falling onto his lab coat like dandruff. He alternated between looking at me and the croissant. "You're with Mr. Angermann, right?"

I nodded.

"He had a spot this morning."

"Excuse me?"

"A spot."

"On his lung?"

"What makes you think that?" The doctor laughed out loud. "No, around his surgical scar. A little spot, not uncommon. Don't worry."

He gave me a friendly pat on the back and disappeared into the building.

In the evening, Elias's scar was weeping. The pus gave off a sweet, biting odor that reminded me of the Soviet perfume Warszawinka and triggered a gag reflex. Elias's camera was lying on the nightstand. He was facing the wall, feverish. We had rung for the nurse, but she took her time and then appeared in the room so suddenly that at first I thought she was a ghost. Wearing a short lab coat, the nurse exposed her teeth. Her yellowish incisor was decorated with a blue rhinestone. Not to be taken seriously. She stood there with her hands on her hips and her head thrown back. Her eyes had a fundamentalist glow to them. In a quick, deep voice she

said that Elias should get up now. I didn't think that
was a good idea. But when she loudly pointed out that
I didn't know what I was talking about, I had to agree.
Although I kept that bit to myself.

The nurse jockeyed Elias out of the bed: "Come on,
young man. Get up!"

Elias bit his lip and stood. I saw the pain in his face
and yelled at the nurse. My words sounded shrill.

"It's for his own good!" she yelled back.

When Elias took a step forward he moaned with
pain, but remained standing. He stood and suffered
and the nurse nodded encouragingly. "Go ahead, go
ahead."

Elias took another step, this time no sound escaped
him. His face was white as a sheet.

"Can't you see that he's in pain?"

"Pain is a part of life. Believe me, I've been working
here twenty years!"

"Twenty years too long!"

"Masha, it's OK!" Elias's forehead shone with little
pearls of sweat, his breathing fast and irregular. He took
a wavering step toward the bed, looking for something
to hold on to, and with an audible gasp he clasped the
bedpost with both hands. I pushed him onto the bed.
Elias gave in to my movements and allowed me to sit
him up. I laid my hand on his cheek, which was rough
and hot. His eyes were filled with tears. As were mine.

I stood in front of Elias, ready for anything. But Elias pulled me down toward him onto the bed and feebly told the nurse: "Please leave."

"That's a first." The woman stormed out, slamming the door shut behind her.

Elias put his head on my shoulder and I helped him to lie down. He got into a fetal position and turned to face the wall. Shortly after, his whole body started shivering. I stroked his hair, but he didn't react. I ran into the hallway and dragged the next nurse who passed by into the room. She removed the dressing from Elias's wound and quickly closed the curtains that separated his bed from the others, even though the other beds were empty. The wound looked bad.

Elias was sent to the radiology ward. When he was brought back, he was convulsing with pain. The doctors were waiting for the lab results. Finally, the senior physician came in, a short bald guy with a paunch. He was followed by a dozen medical students, because this turned out to be a teaching hospital. The senior physician examined the wound, furrowing his brow. Afterward the students hunkered over Elias. Some assumed a disgusted expression, others pushed their colleagues aside to get a better look. I stood in the corner and refused to look at both Elias and the wound. I could smell it.

Elias, pale and no longer responsive, was wheeled back into the operating theater early in the morning. His parents had left home before dawn. Now we were all waiting in the cafeteria: his father with his large-pored nose and brutish face, his mother, chubby cheeks and robust arms. Both sat silently in front of full mugs and homemade sandwiches.

Horst read *Der Spiegel* while Elke and I looked out the window. The sky was dreary. The weather had turned windy and rainy overnight. The father and mother took turns covertly examining me. I looked at their faces and was reminded of Elias's childhood pictures: first day at school, Elias in front of the Christmas tree, at his civic initiation ceremony—a pale and shy child. When they both happened to be looking at me at the same time, I suddenly felt embarrassed about my clothes, for having put on makeup and for wearing heels—despite the fact that I had spent the night at the hospital and that it hadn't been this morning when I'd put on the makeup, but the morning before. Elke cleared her throat and checked her watch, Horst nervously rustled the magazine.

The window where we were sitting was facing the narrow and empty street. A gray bundle in the middle of the road caught my eye. At first I thought it was just a plastic bag, but plastic bags are rarely gray. Then I thought it was a stuffed animal. I excused myself, setting my mug on the table a little too loudly, and said I had to use the restroom. In the restroom the mirror reflected a rather unpleasant image: my nose was shiny, which made it look bigger and bumpier than usual. My mascara was smudged. The doctor couldn't tell how long the surgery would take.

I was standing out on the street and kept my breathing low to calm myself. The wind was icy and my hands shivered. For a while I monitored my breathing, then I spotted the animal. A rabbit. And it was alive. At least its ribcage rose and fell in irregular intervals. I knew only two prayers: the Lord's Prayer and Shema Yisrael. The Lord's Prayer was useless and Shema Yisrael by itself wouldn't be sufficient. I would bargain with God. Elias versus the rabbit. HE should let the rabbit die and not Elias. I deeply regretted not being religious and not having anything more impressive up my sleeve than "Hear, O Israel: the Lord is our God, the Lord is one. You shall love the Lord your God with all your heart, with all your soul, and with all your might. These words which I command you today shall be on your heart." I swayed in prayer as I had seen the Orthodox Jews do on one of the public channels. Not Elias.

Please not him. Not him. Not him. I would bury the rabbit and recite the rabbit kaddish by heart.

I told God that HE could kill the rabbit right away. The rabbit kept breathing, no car in sight. I carefully lifted the rabbit. It didn't have any exterior wounds, but its ears hung limply, its fur full of street dust and its red eyes as good as dead (insofar as death can be predicted from red eye color). And what if it wasn't hurt? What if it was just lying down for a quick rest?

I put the rabbit back down and once again recited the Shema Yisrael. On the right a small GM Opel passed by. Elias's parents were watching me from the cafeteria window. Panic rose inside me, I searched for a stone. The thought "There are no stones here" passed through my head. But Elias's life was at stake. I walked along the street and next to the bus stop there was a stone. A good sign. I climbed over the guard rail and took the first stone that I found.

When I returned, the animal had remained persistently alive. How do you explain faith to a rabbit? I bent down to pat its head—it was soft and wet and didn't react to my touch. My hand shook. I stood up, took aim. The stone hit the ground next to the rabbit's head. Again I lifted the stone and had the distinct feeling that the rabbit was staring at me. I asked it for forgiveness and once more let go of the stone. This time I hit the mark and its skull burst. The brain mass leaked and mixed with blood and bone splinters. I turned away and suppressed a rising sickness.

As I returned to the cafeteria and to Elias's parents, I tried to tread lightly and not to let my heels clatter too loudly on the marble steps. My hands were red from the cold.

The surgery had been successful, Resident Physician Weiss informed us. He stood there bow-legged and grinning, shaking Horst's and Elke's hands. I stood by their side, looking at Elias. He lay motionless in his bed. An even longer piece of metal protruded from his thigh. In three weeks, approximately, he would be allowed to return home. He could then continue the treatment as an outpatient. The rain pattered against the window and out on the street. Pedestrians under umbrellas were trying to outrun the weather.

3

My mother kept calling and asking whether I wanted her to visit, and I kept saying no. She came on Sunday and brought the leftovers of my father's birthday dinner. I put two plates out, as well as forks and knives. I left the food itself in the Tupperware containers, not bothering to reheat it. Mother gave me a concerned look and I stared back wearily. She wanted to know everything about Elisha's diagnosis. My parents had long agonized over how to Russify Elias's name, to impose both their love and an affectionate diminutive on him. When my father finally exclaimed "Elisha," my mother applauded in delight—Elisha it was.

We ate in silence. I didn't mind it, but my mother couldn't bear the quiet and started talking about her job. She was a piano teacher—first at a music school, then at an academy. She, too, initially struggled with the new system: trained at a Soviet conservatory, she had professional standards which she couldn't just leave behind. When the father of one of her students, a priest, complained to her that his daughter didn't have fun in class, my mother's heart started racing and her hands grew sweaty. Thus far she had not been aware that the purpose of art was *fun*. And she would've least expected to hear it from a priest. Music had been taken very seriously in the USSR, as were ballet and the visual arts. Unlike in Germany, every child had the opportunity to get not only a school education, but also a highly professional and—on top of that—free artistic education, as long as the child was willing to work hard. And it was completely unfathomable to my mother how somebody could not want that.

Back in the day, when she was still young, gorgeous, and successful, and before she married my father on a whim, our living room had held a grand piano. Preparing for a performance, my mother would practice for days on end. Because of hygienic concerns and the General Situation, I'd only gone to kindergarten for a few weeks. Instead, I'd stayed in the living room, sitting under the grand piano and listening to my mother play.

Whenever I saw my parents now, I always assured them that I was fine. I talked about my stipends, summer academies, internships, and stays abroad. I told them about my plans; where I would work and how much I would earn. I told them about Sami and then about Elias, and my parents believed every single word because I played my role well. When we got around to the meat dish, lamb with steamed chestnuts, dried fruit, and dolma (those grape leaves stuffed with rice, ground lamb, finely minced onions, and nuts), my mother laughed. I told her hospital anecdotes that I made up as I went along.

She finally left, leaving behind pomegranates, oranges, pears, bananas, stuffed puff pastry, and the last piece of chocolate cake. I turned on the TV. A rerun episode of *Tatort* flickered across the screen. All signs pointed toward the detective spending a hot night with a Southern European. I cranked up the volume and went off to take a shower. I thoroughly scrubbed away dead skin cells and the faint smell of hospital. I tried to recall Elias's body without the screws and the long scar on his thigh. Then I imagined kissing a woman in the staircase, in the midst of banging doors, cooking smells, and screaming children, and how I would slip my hands between her thighs. I was back on the couch, putting cream on my legs, before the murderer was caught. I had a suspicion and awaited the solution.

———————

The digital display on the clock radio showed four a.m. My stomach cramped, I had a bad taste in my mouth, my neck ached. Grudgingly I schlepped myself to the bathroom and looked for the tampon box. Under the warm stream of the shower I washed off the blood, then wrapped myself in a mint green towel and went back to bed.

It was quiet in the apartment. I wondered whether I had locked the front door, whether it was normal that the fridge made such dubious noises and why the neighbors were already awake, stomping down the stairs. At five a.m. I decided that staying in bed was pointless. I picked up the first piece of clothing I found, a red-and-white-checkered summer dress that barely covered my hips so that I looked like a child that had grown too quickly. I tied my hair back and went into the kitchen. I tried to imagine all the things I could do now that Elias wasn't there, but couldn't come up with any. And therefore I also stopped doing the things I used to do in his presence: every surface was cluttered with open packaging, newspapers, used mugs, bowls; the trash was overflowing and of course I'd not bothered to separate out paper, plastic, compost, metal, electronic appliances, and bulky items. I turned on the radio and translated the morning news into French while I rinsed out the stovetop espresso maker and soaked a crescent roll in a bowl of milk. The phone's ringing startled me and I choked on the roll, which I hadn't bothered to bake prior to consumption. The display showed Elisha's number.

"Already awake?" I asked, surprised.

"What do you think? They wake us up at six a.m. for the ward round and stare at us like rabbits pulled out of a hat. And if somebody sleeps through the magic trick, they'll come back."

"How are you?"

The line crackled.

"Are you in pain?" I asked again.

"No," he replied.

Both of us knew this was a lie.

"Do you think you could come earlier today?" he hesitantly asked.

"Yes." I tried to sound tender, and just then recalled that I had a seminar today. But it was too late. I had already agreed to come.

"Thank you."

"No problem. Should I bring you anything?"

"Warm clothes—I have to keep the windows open here." He murmured something into the telephone that I didn't understand and then continued in a normal volume: "A scarf and a pullover if possible, the black one and the light gray cashmere one."

"Do you want anything to eat?"

"God no. I'm constantly being force-fed here. I'm starting to beef up. But you could bring me the books and the lens from the dresser, first drawer on the left. This time the right one, please."

"You hardly need all your fucking equipment there, do you?"

I hung up and tried to fish the soggy piece of bread from the cereal bowl. It turned out to be easier to just drink everything. I was furious. With Elias, with myself, with the entire world.

I wandered through the art academy library that was so very different from the one in my department. Again and again I pulled a book from the shelves and leafed through reproductions of old Flemish masters and descriptions of happenings. Holding in my hands the catalog for the Sonic Youth exhibition, I asked myself whether my life had taken the right course. Languages come easily to me. I quickly grasp the patterns and have a good memory, but in the last few years I had hardly done anything other than learn technical terms and grammar constructions. I was disciplined and hungry for success. In school I had studied English, French, and a bit of Italian, then I had spent a year as an au pair in France to perfect my French. Afterward, I'd enrolled to study interpreting. In my free time I studied Italian,

Spanish, and a bit of Polish, but I never managed to work up enthusiasm for the Slavic languages. Nonetheless, I spent a semester at the Lomonosov University in Moscow, then did internships with international organizations in Brussels, Vienna, and Warsaw. A scholarship had freed me from having to work on the side. But by then I had compiled a respectable CV and was familiar with the use of Ritalin and other substances that facilitate an easier learning process. I finished college in record time and started taking Arabic lessons. Sami had been a good teacher, but he returned to the United States. A year later I met Elias.

We'd been together for a mere two months when we decided to travel together. We were on the road for almost four months, crossed France, into Italy, from there on to the Balearic Islands and Spain, then to Morocco, Egypt, and Turkey. During the trip Elias took pictures for his thesis show. Upon our return he disappeared into his darkroom and I started a double master's degree: interpretation and Arabic.

The librarian wore large horn-rimmed glasses and stared at my T-shirt. I pushed the books toward him. "I'm sorry, I can't help it. They're beautiful. Your breasts, I mean."

I looked him straight in the eyes—they were cold and gray. Obviously he was at ease, didn't feel embarrassed or caught in the act, and smilingly handed me

the books. Probably he had deconstructed his own sex-
ism and now felt that he could get away with anything.
I was tempted to drop the heavy stack of art monographs onto his fingers, but he withdrew his hands just
in time. Then I thought about spitting at him, but that
seemed a little overly theatrical.

I was so angry that I walked the entire way to the university. I hoped that would calm me down. On foot it
took an hour. I had to cross the crowded downtown
and financial districts. En route I was asked to donate
money three times, smiled at six times, two people
asked for a cigarette, three people asked me for a euro,
and an aging hippie asked me to give him a tantra
massage. I was too late for my seminar and my French
translation was subadequate. In general, I wasn't in the
mood for *Simultaneous Interpretation French–German
III* and *Introduction à la problématique des techniques
industrielles.* Or any translation for that matter.

My professor asked me to come to his office hours.
Over the course of my studies I had never gotten
worse than a 3.7 and that was by accident in the first
semester. This afternoon he would be sitting across
from me, stirring his spoon around his blue mug and
asking me to work harder. Then he would inquire

about vineyards in Azerbaijan and would pity me for
becoming multilingual so late in life. I would never
be a native speaker, nothing to be done about that.
And I would remain silent and stir my unsweetened
tea and not mention the superb cognac from Ganja.
A cognac that is available neither in an elegant bottle nor at a fancy specialty shop on Fressgass Street,
but only in Ganja and only in small canisters that are
mailed exclusively to real connoisseurs or close relatives. I furthermore would abstain from mentioning
that I didn't learn Azerbaijani from my parents, but
from our neighbors, and that I'd spoken it fluently
and without an accent until we emigrated to Germany, where I no longer had a reason to speak it in
my daily life anymore. And I would leave him in the
dark about the fact that in Azerbaijan, starting at age
five, I had a private tutor in English and French and
that my mother had to sell her mother's diamond ring
to pay for it. I wouldn't tell him that people who live
without running water aren't necessarily uneducated.
But my professor was my professor. He sponsored fos-
ter children in Africa and India. His multiculturalism
took place in congress halls, convention centers, and
expensive hotels. To him integration meant demand-
ing fewer hijabs and more skin, hunting for exclusive
wines and exotic travel destinations.

When I arrived at the hospital I was even angrier. Rainer said that Elias was in the middle of an examination. Heinz added, winking: "It might take a while. But don't worry, stay with us. We'll take care of you." Both laughed.

I slammed my books on the table and went straight back out. There was a little park between the different wards, but it wasn't quiet there either. The benches were constantly occupied by old people, the narrow paths congested with wheelchairs. I sat down on the only free bench and lit a cigarette. Not five minutes later a delicate old lady with a colorful hijab and golden front teeth sat down next to me. From her hospital pajamas she produced a bag of sunflower seeds, cracked them in her mouth, and spit the empty shells onto the ground directly in front of my feet.

"It's not allowed inside anymore. The neighbors complain to the doctor."

I replied in Russian, and her face lit up. She waved the bag of sunflower seeds in my face.

"Do you have a fiancé?"

"No."

"A boyfriend?"

I nodded. She spit out a bunch of empty shells, satisfied.

"When I was your age I was already married."

I shrugged.

"How often?"

"Excuse me?"

"How often?" She repeated. "How often does he hit you? Does he hit hard, with full force?"

"He doesn't."

"Everybody hits. My husband hit me. My mother-in-law. She, she hit the hardest. She was quite a hitter, that one. But my daughter-in-law was bad, too. I was in a hospital for two years."

"Two years?"

"Yes. Two years."

"Was it a locked ward?"

"Of course not, I'm perfectly clear in the head. What are you talking about? I was pregnant. With my seventh."

I said nothing.

"As if six weren't enough. I told him not to touch me anymore, but he kept on doing it anyway."

I nodded.

"I didn't want anymore. I went up on top of the closet and jumped. The abdominal organs fell out and here I was. And now I'm here again."

4

I knew the man who knelt by the cash register to pick up his change. Black coat, silver hair arranged neatly around his square head. I didn't notice him right away. Only later did I recognize his teetering gait and the pointy tips of his crocodile leather shoes. At school he passed us smilingly, the way you might pass a group of people whose faces you don't need to discern. Windmill gave consultations and embodied the arrogance of a successful interpreter who wore the starched collar of his shirts turned up, spoke multiple languages to perfection, and got assignments from all the big institutions. Rumor had it that his voice was so agreeable over headphones that at one point he'd received a suggestive offer from a delegate of Liechtenstein. In most of his lectures he reached a state of ultimate self-reference.

Windmill stood at the register and paid for a sandwich. There was nothing but a cemetery, a funeral home, and a drugstore near the Northwest Hospital. I sat in the hospital cafeteria facing a watery soup that I couldn't bring myself to eat. I kept imagining which bacteria were swimming among the overcooked potatoes and canned carrots. Elias had been in the orthopedic ward for two weeks and still had at least that long to go. We counted the days. The number seemed large or small depending on the mood.

Windmill gave me a smile. I cautiously smiled back. He came over and asked whether he could sit with me. All the other tables in the cafeteria were unoccupied. I nodded.

"You know what? I think we've met before."

Again, I nodded.

"You were one of my students, weren't you?" He smiled encouragingly. "Why did you drop out of my seminar?" He took a bite of his sandwich.

I remained silent.

"Russian?"

"A bit."

I was about to elaborate, but Windmill waved dismissively and said, "I'd rather hear about your B-languages."

"Russian, French, and English."

"Any others?"

"Not as working languages."

"But I'm sure you have C-options."

I nodded and didn't know what to say. Windmill peered at me. I nodded again and stared into my cup.

On my third day in Germany I went to school and was promptly demoted by two grades. Instead of practicing algebra I was supposed to color mandalas with crayons.

I accompanied my parents to the immigration office and there learned that language meant power. If you didn't speak any German you had no voice. And if you only spoke a little you went unheard. Applications were accepted and dismissed according to accent. We waited until my parents' number came up on the monitor above the heavy iron door. The wait was usually very long. The immigration office rarely managed to process more than five migrants a day, and we had to stand in line hours before opening to have a chance at getting our turn before closing time. I also accompanied my mother to parent-teacher meetings—a thoroughly tormenting affair. I sat next to her in the hallway, sporting a bowl cut, substantial eyeglasses, and braces. I stared at my feet and took turns being embarrassed about my mother and myself. The German, math, and geography teachers announced unanimously that my language skills were subpar and that I was out of place at this high school. Impatiently I translated this for my mother. The high school that I attended knew immigrants solely from tabloid papers and afternoon TV shows. In my class there was a girl whose mother was from Finland and in my year a boy whose mother was Dutch, but neither of them wore clothes purchased at the discount store, and both were Mormons anyway. There were no Arabs, blacks, or Turks. I trudged behind my classmates, tried to acquire the same clothing style and hobbies, neither of which we could afford. When the class was too loud I was blamed, despite the fact that I was too ashamed to open my mouth. For three years I hardly spoke a word and instead focused on a vague idea of "later." I wove dreams: studied maps, read travel guides, and made lists of things I would need on my travels. I was sure that everything would be better once I left and started living, as a photographer, journalist, or stewardess. Our small town had an American military base and sometimes I thought about marrying a soldier. But I didn't find myself pretty enough and later I learned that the soldiers' wives stayed in Germany. But I wanted to leave.

In the eleventh grade I had a German teacher who suffered from hair loss. Neither her colleagues nor her students forgave her for that. When she couldn't take the humiliation any longer, she passed it on. It was a quiet, wan winter afternoon in the airless classroom. The German teacher also taught social studies and we were on the topic of immigrant delinquency. Everybody was in favor of immediate deportation of criminal aliens. Specifically, we were talking about the Mehmet case. Although I wouldn't want to run into this Mehmet guy in a dark alley, I failed to grasp what set him apart from German criminals. He'd been born in Germany, raised in Munich, and attended only German public schools. The only difference was he didn't have German citizenship. My teacher made sure to tell us exactly what was wrong with him.

When I couldn't take the discussion any longer, I took my craft scissors out of my pencil case and approached the teacher. I stood facing her, scissors in my right hand. At that moment, I knew I could do anything I wanted. I tore the wig from her head. Somebody gave a loud laugh as her scalp was revealed, almost bald with only a few streaks of limp hair. She didn't resist. Just looked at me, shocked. I pitied her, because—like me—she was a victim. But unlike her I'd decided to defend myself.

I was expelled. My mother was horrified, my father amused and a little bit proud. I knew that now everything would get better. At first I wanted to give up school altogether and instead go on a trip around the world, but I had neither the money nor a German passport. Therefore, I switched over to the Max Beckmann School in Frankfurt and moved in with Sibel. I was seventeen.

Now I spoke five languages fluently and a few others like white trash Germans speak German. But I didn't have anything that resembled free time.

"What are you doing here?" Windmill asked.

"I'm visiting my boyfriend."

He nodded and didn't ask about Elias, which was all right by me.

"And you?" I asked.

"I'm going to give you my card. Let me know if I can help with anything."

Even after Windmill had long finished his meal and left I still held his card in my hand.

5

The room was overheated and stuffy. Elias didn't say a word and neither did I. Heinz had been released a couple of days ago and Rainer was being examined.

"I would cover it with a blanket if I could," said Elias.

I pulled my knees to my chest and rested my head on them, a position in which I saw neither Elias nor his wound.

"Are you not going to look at me until I'm completely healed?"

"I just can't look at your leg."

"Why not?"

I paced the room. Elias followed me with his desperate, tired eyes. Still, at his core he was healthy, and I envied him this. He lowered his gaze.

"I don't know how long I'll be able to bear this," he said.

"Are you breaking up with me?"

"I can't help you."

"Did I ask for your help?"

"Why don't you finally tell me what happened to you? You didn't emigrate until 1996. And by then, you didn't really have to anymore."

"Didn't really have to anymore? What do you know?"

"Exactly. What do I know?" Elias repeated bitterly.

"You sound like the immigration office," I said, interrupting him.

He took a deep breath and said, "It's impossible to have a relationship like this."

"So, that's it? You're breaking up with me?" I yelled.

"No!"

"Then none of this bullshit."

I stormed out and slammed the door behind me. We had this conversation rather frequently and it got worse every time.

In the restroom I held my hands under the warm water. First the backs, then the wrists, until finally I held my head under the jet. Water dripped onto my feet. I thought about running away. It would take me two hours to pack and be out of the apartment. I could survive in most countries. Actually, now that I thought about it, I didn't really need anything. I could just go.

I went back in. Elias smiled and reached out for me. I took a step closer to the bed. The sun died in the sky and flooded the room with warm light.

"There was a child and a father. The father wanted to bring the child to safety. It was a ten-minute walk to her grandmother's apartment. The child wasn't even seven years old and she felt that something had changed over the past few days, but couldn't say what. That was what the child was thinking about when next to her a woman hit the asphalt. The pool of blood slowly reached the child's shoes and the tips of the shoes soaked up the red. The blood was warm and the woman was younger than I am today. The child pushed back a strand of hair and a bit of blood remained on her cheek. It could have been worse, the grandmother said later that evening, as she cleaned the bloody crust off the child's shoes."

Elias took my hand in his, kissed my palm, and covered my arm with small kisses. Then he reached out for my face, stroked my cheek, and pulled me in close.

6

The sky was gloomy and commuters waited on the plat-
form. Completely identical groups of students entered
and exited. The S-Bahn stopped every two minutes.
I couldn't concentrate on my flash cards and instead
observed the students. The boys were dressed in public housing fashion. The girls utilized their cellphone
screens as mirrors and tried to fix their hairstyles.
The gangsta peer group boasted with Turkish-Arabic
pseudo-syntax. The underage ones bid their fellow students goodbye with "OK then . . . *bunun üzerine,* bye."
Fields, new buildings, and train stations now only appeared from time to time and they yelled at each other.
"OK, like, bye!" Houses and people started to look like

loaves of bread that had not fully risen. I was glad that my youth was over.

Officially, we were part of a contingent of Jewish refugees that were allotted to strengthen the Jewish communities in Germany. But our emigration had nothing to do with Judaism and everything to do with Nagorno-Karabakh.

In the beginning of 1987, a campaign was launched in Armenia to integrate Nagorno-Karabakh into the Armenian Soviet Republic. At that time, both Azeris and Armenians lived in the territory. Mass demonstrations by Armenians were held in Yerevan, the first of their kind in the Soviet Union. On February 20, 1988, the Nagorno-Karabakh Autonomous Oblast declared their secession from the Azerbaijan Soviet Republic. Clashes followed, and the first wave of Azeris had to flee. Then the situation escalated. But nobody expected the Sumgait Massacre. It all started with a small demonstration. Supposedly it was Azeri refugees from Kafan who had gathered in the city center. The police didn't do anything. Over the next two days, multiple Azeri gangs raided the city and turned it into a death zone for Armenians: they broke windows, set cars on fire, and looked for Armenians. Apartments were trashed and plundered, the residents debased, abused, and raped.

Several people were mutilated with axes—to the point that their bodies couldn't be identified later. The murderers often couldn't tell Azeris from Armenians as there were no distinguishing ethnic features and most Armenians spoke excellent Azerbaijani. I was on my way to the conservatory with my mother when the first rumors reached Baku. We were standing in the line for bread and the woman in front of us told another woman in Russian that her friends' car had been stopped, the passengers had been ordered to get out and recite the Azerbaijani word for hazelnut—*fundukh*. "Say *fundukh*!" the attacker yelled. "If you can say *fundukh* you are a Muslim. Then you have nothing to worry about." My mother explained to me that Azeris and Armenians pronounced the word differently. That was the only explanation she could give. About thirty people died during the pogrom. Almost all 14,000 inhabitants of Armenian descent fled from Sumgait.

Over the next months and years there was to be more violence, displacements, rapes, and pogroms on both sides. The national movements gained backing, the status of Nagorno-Karabakh remained unresolved. Then the Armenian parliament decided that Nagorno-Karabakh belonged to Armenia. Two days later the Azeris declared that it was, in fact, their land. Armenians left Azerbaijan and Azeris left Armenia, and few did so by choice. We collected clothes and food for the ever-increasing number of refugees. The first time I saw a boy my age begging in the city center with stumps instead of legs, I was infuriated because I understood that this wasn't the result of an accident, nor had he been born that way. My father was sent to Karabakh as an observer and often for days on end we didn't know whether he was still alive.

The fight for power and oil was raging. In Baku the National Front was founded. Meetings were held in factories and offices. Arms, purchased from Russian soldiers (illegally, of course), were stashed away. Back then, a Kalashnikov was a hundred dollars, a tank three thousand. Our neighbor became a fervent nationalist, too. When she attended assemblies my mother watched her son Farid.

The hatred was nothing personal. It was structural. The people didn't have faces anymore. No eyes, no names, and no professions—they became Azeris, Armenians, Georgians, and Russians. People who'd been acquainted all their lives forgot everything about each other. Only their alleged nationality remained.

On January 13, 1990, members of the National Front, refugees from the annexed territories, and supposed KGB agents went from one Armenian apartment to the next. There was a system to it. They had lists with Armenian addresses. Their visits meant looting, rape, mutilation, and murder. They killed people with knives and sticks. It wasn't uncommon for people to fall out of windows. I was not allowed to leave the house or ask questions.

My grandfather, who was living with us at the time, was a dark-eyed, dark-haired man with pronounced cheekbones. In the tram, on his way to the university, where he taught inorganic chemistry, he was taken for an Armenian and beaten up. Three days later he died of a heart attack. I found him that morning in his favorite chair. My father locked the door to his room. It had been his father.

My mother, drenched in tears, called her mother. They argued for a while until my mother hung up and told me to get dressed. She packed a bag and handed it to my father. It was quiet in the streets. Next to some houses lay smashed furniture. And glass. My father dragged me by the arm, told me to hurry up. My grandmother lived only three streets away. When I arrived at her apartment my childhood was over.

On January 15, 1991, Russian troops gathered around Baku. The population grew nervous. Roadblocks and barriers were erected on roads leading to Baku and in front of Russian barracks. The Russian invasion had to be stopped. A few days later the radio and TV stations were blown up by a KGB unit. Static on all channels. Nobody knew anything anymore and we were prepared for everything. I heard the first tanks roll down the streets. Our neighbor stood in my parents' kitchen and yelled: "All Russians are murderers." Calm and composed, my father answered, "Please leave my house."

Russian snipers shot at unarmed people. Tanks rolled over barricades, over people, over an ambulance. Hundreds died that night. A sixteen-year-old Jewish girl was shot in her living room because her shadow was visible on the window. She bled to death lying on a rug in colors and ornamentation typical of the Caucasus region.

The next morning tens of thousands demonstrated in front of the president's palace. On January 23 there was a rally for the fallen martyrs and my parents tried to bury my grandfather at it. His corpse had been decaying in our apartment for days. The decision turned out to be a bad one. My parents' car was stopped, they were accused of being Russian agents and murderers and almost dragged out of the car. The target of the hatred now was Russians. My parents were accompanied by a friend who spoke accent-free Azerbaijani and was a member of the National Front. This friend saved my parents' lives that day.

A general strike marked the following forty days of mourning. The declaration of independence followed in October. Instruments for identification and classification were created; a new flag flew: blue, red, and green with a white crescent and a white eight-pointed star. Blue represented the sky, red freedom and the blood that was shed to gain the freedom, green the fertility of the land—all of which we learned at school. I didn't start school until December. We kept our coats on in the classroom and wrote with gloves because the windows were broken. An unannounced curfew descended over Baku like fog and would remain there until our emigration.

Nagorno-Karabakh was at war. Our neighbor implored God five times a day: "Don't let my son go." It didn't help. Farid was drafted two days after his eighteenth birthday. My mother gave him my father's warm jacket. Farid didn't return and his mother stopped praying.

Refugees from Nagorno-Karabakh camped out in parks, wrapped in blankets. Some of them were mutilated. Many occupied Armenian apartments, by force if necessary. A million Azeris had fled from Nagorno-Karabakh. The schools with classes in Azerbaijani filled with new students from Karabakh, while the Russian-speaking ones emptied out. Meanwhile, I played with my dolls and practiced forgetting.

In the following years there was hardly any gas, hardly any electricity, hardly any water, at most for an hour a day. Every hospital treatment came at a price. Money couldn't be printed fast enough and any semblance of comprehensible rules had gone out the window. The system had collapsed. People who recently had been well off now hurried along the streets, cowering, their expressions desperate. Many took to begging. A well-dressed woman rang our doorbell. Her twins were dying. Her hands shook as she took my mother's money. The intelligentsia and the mafia left. Hardly anybody stayed in Baku: no doctors, no professors, no engineers; neither Armenians, nor Georgians, Jews, Russians, Tartars. The only thing left was graves. Relatives from abroad sent money for their upkeep.

We couldn't stay in Azerbaijan.

My father refused to go to Israel. Every morning my mother spoke about the anti-Semitism in Russia, but in private couldn't imagine my father living in a Jewish state either. Besides, the words *Occupied Territories*, *army*, and *Jewish state* didn't quite fit her utopia.

In 1990 my aunt immigrated to Israel. My parents didn't go along. Both had good jobs and decided to wait. At first there was the hope of getting into the United States or Canada, but those borders were the first to close. The remaining options were Germany and Israel, but only as a Jew, and thus the register in the synagogue filled up, as did the immigration applications at the German and Israeli embassies. The same people who were bribed to erase the word *Jew* from passports and birth certificates in the past were now bribed to do the opposite.

In the meantime, the Gulf War broke out. Iraq launched Scud missiles against Israel and my mother sat in front of the TV, desperate, telephone in hand. Of course that was useless as international calls had to be ordered weeks in advance.

My relatives spent their first Israeli winter in bunkers wearing gas masks. My mother decided that she wouldn't under any circumstances follow them. Initially the idea to go to Germany of all places seemed just as absurd to my parents. In 1994 my mother still claimed that she would never set foot in this country—the ashes were still warm. My grandmother was a survivor. Nine months later, my parents filed an application for emigration at the German embassy. In 1995 the application was approved and we began selling our things: first household electronics and kitchen equipment, then the furniture. My mother didn't have long to think about whom to leave her grand piano. Every sale was celebrated with a meal. Food was available again, if at exorbitant prices. Only the books didn't find a new owner. The two thousand volumes made for a big heap of trash. In 1996 we were in Germany. In 1997, for the first time, I considered suicide.

———

Friedberg was the final stop. I got off. The weather was bad, the houses low and quiet. In front of the train station it smelled like urine and a twelve-year-old yelled "cunt" in my direction. As I turned around to face him, he laughed out loud and said something in Turkish to his friends, who wolfed down stir-fried noodles in front of a Chinese take-out shop. Now the whole group erupted in roaring laughter and I wished for them to choke on their food.

The bell gave three loud shrieks before my father opened the door. The corners of his mouth briefly twitched in surprise before resuming their usual disheartened expression. My father was a man who had understood that things would never be good. I tolerated his lips brushing my right cheek and carefully patted his back. He told me that my mother wasn't home and wanted to know if I had eaten. Not awaiting my reply he went back up into the bedroom, to his computer and his Russian movies. I took one of my mother's lactose-free yogurts from the fridge and sat down in front of the TV, but didn't turn it on.

The dark brown leather sofa was covered with a beige throw. The remote control was wrapped in plastic foil.

The wall shelves featured, next to the Russian edition of the complete works of Feuchtwanger, framed photos of better days: my mother and I at the beach in front of a sandcastle; my grandparents' wedding picture; my father as a young man, at the gate of the Yuri Gagarin Training Center. All Russians wanted to be cosmonauts, but my father actually was one. Just one who never got to go into space. Father was a member of the Communist Party, just like Yuri Gagarin. He graduated from flight school with honors, studied—like Gagarin—at the military academy for air force engineers in Moscow, completed the cosmonaut training—like Gagarin—but that's where their parallel story ends. Nobody knew why. Father returned to Baku, and nobody resented him for this setback, nobody saw his return as defeat. He got a post at the ministry and became a respected and very busy man. I think that and the collapse of the Soviet Union were the big surprises in his life.

Sometimes when he got home from work he took me up to the roof. There he set up a telescope and explained the constellations to me, whispered their names into my ear, as if we were the only two people who knew those names, as if they were a secret between us. I felt his warm breath, smelling of almonds, and if father had had a drink before, he'd bring me to bed, let me change into my nightgown, give me a kiss, his beard stubble brushing against my cheek, and stroke my hair. Then he'd lay his hand on the radiator just as gently as he had touched my head earlier and leave the room.

Germany had no use for my father. In his social Siberia he wore jogging pants and those undershirts that are called *wife beaters* (not that he ever did). From one day to the next, Father had given up. He didn't befriend other people. He rarely left the house, and if so, it was mostly to compare prices at gas stations.

Mother went to the kitchen first. Father came down, took a seat at the table, and started stuffing cigarettes. In a sweeping action, Mother opened the fridge door. My job was to squeeze a lemon and dice an onion. She heated olive oil in a heavy cast iron pan and searched for rosemary. Father waited impatiently until the fish had gained a golden-brown crust and opened a bottle of wine. At the dinner table my mother sometimes talked about her piano students. My father and I took turns asking questions when the silence became unbearable. During dessert my father listed all his acquaintances who had ever broken a bone and my mother corrected him every time. Her eyes were as big and dangerous as headlights.

I had wanted to leave the next morning, but mother was already defrosting the lamb for dinner. I didn't dare to go. The second evening got melancholic. My parents sat on the couch and reminisced about the glimmering surface of the water in the bay of Baku, the tour boats, and Rostropovich's performances. Almost all the memories they'd kept were pleasant. They had intentionally forgotten about the corruption, the National Front, the lines in front of empty grocery stores and Western embassies, often stretching several kilometers long. On the other hand, the memories of the lines amused my mother, as did those of the home for asylum seekers and the Baltic herring. Back then, a major part of our diet consisted of the aforementioned Baltic herring as well as illegally fished and processed caviar. But you couldn't get bread or anything else—just Baltic herring. I would stand in line with my mother for hours to get them. In candlelight—electricity had become rare, as had candles, actually—my mother gutted the fish with her pianist hands.

When I returned to Frankfurt two days later, I had three bottles of kosher wine in my bag. My mother never drank this wine. She ordered it through the synagogue, to do the rabbi and God a favor, only to then order twice the amount of Georgian wine from her friends. The market-based correlation between the sale of kosher wine through the synagogue and that of Georgian wine in the community center was striking.

7

Even the floor-to-ceiling windows along one wall couldn't brighten the dark wood-paneled interior of the room. On the bar stood a vase with lilies. The wall to the right sported a flat-screen TV that showed CNN on mute. During lunch hour the bar was always crowded with bankers who spoke English with European accents, loosened their ties, and ordered sandwiches.

Cem stared at the TV. The cafe had only opened half an hour ago. The waiter stood listlessly behind the bar and polished glasses with a checkered dish towel. His jaw-length hair fell into his face.

"You look pale," Cem said.

The top buttons of his shirt were open, a golden

crescent glistened on his chest. Cem had an uneven growth of beard, with a hairless patch on his right cheek.

I sat down across from him. He was the first person in his family to go to university and speak better Turkish than his parents. Cem had been born in Frankfurt and raised bilingually. At least that's what he thought. It wasn't until a vacation in Istanbul that he realized that he had a strong dialect. He often had to search for words. And so he spent a year at Istanbul's best university and acquired the refined accent of the city's upper class. With his relatives he kept speaking in the dialect of the village they came from before moving to Germany. We spoke German with each other—two perfectly integrated model foreigners. As Azerbaijani and Turkish are similar enough that we could understand each other, I told him in my language of the practical jokes we played as kids, and he imitated his parents' or aunts' Turkish. Sometimes he laughed about the archaic terms that I used, deducing them from Azerbaijani.

"What are you drinking?" I asked.

"Whiskey."

"Isn't it a little early for that?"

"*Çüş*."

"When's your exam?"

"In four days, but we're partying tonight."

"I don't want to."

"Of course you want to. You've been in the hospital all day. Tonight you're going out with me. Come on, you need it just as much as I do." He grinned and downed his drink. "But first, take a look at my translation."

The waiter put two glasses and a bowl of peanuts on our table. Cem shot a longing glance at his unopened pack of cigarettes. The package warned of death. I knew that Cem was imagining the crackling noise of the plastic wrap, the tearing of the silver paper, the taste of the filter in his mouth, the click of the lighter, and the first inhale. But maybe he was just thinking of the waiter.

"How is he?" asked Cem.

"Elisha? Crappy. He's in a lot of pain. I try to distract him, but it doesn't work."

"Does he get on your nerves?"

"What kind of a question is that?"

"Well, does he?"

I took a peanut, felt the salty taste on my tongue, and chewed it up.

"I'm sorry," said Cem.

CNN was reporting on the Middle East. A demonstration with angry men wearing keffiyehs and waving Palestinian flags marched through Gaza. Interspersed were sequences with destroyed houses and Israeli tanks. Cem shook his head and took a sip.

"What's going on?" I asked.

He inhaled through his nose and answered: "War."

"I don't think so," I said. Cem looked at me, amused. I added: "We won't know if there'll be war until there's a long talk with a correspondent."

"Looks like there will be. My father already talked about donating for refugees."

"Doesn't he say that every time?" My voice sounded more aggressive than I had intended.

"Exactly." Cem stretched his back, turned his head left and right. His neck cracked loudly. He glanced at the TV, yawned. "Exactly," he repeated. "In the end, Dad prefers to spend the money on lottery tickets anyway." Cem laughed joylessly.

"They always show the same thing," I said. "Just look at it. Pictures of victims and aggressors in a quick sequence. First the text: the Israeli actions are aggressive and disproportionate. And they go deep into Palestinian territory. Then pictures of victims: maltreated mothers crying for their martyrs on the sunbaked ground, blazing fires and Israeli tanks and checkpoints off in the distance."

"And you? You think all of that isn't real? Don't be so naive," he said. CNN showed a blond American journalist gesticulating with concern into the camera.

"The journalists aren't even allowed to enter the territory. They stand on the hill in front of it."

"And write whatever the Israeli military dictates," came Cem's cynical response.

"If they don't speak Hebrew or Arabic—"

"Well, they should take you, then, shouldn't they?" he interrupted.

"Asshole."

"Don't get so worked up over it. Not everybody's underqualified just because they don't have a double major."

I got up and went to the bathroom. I held my hands under the warm water and tried to localize my anger. I felt like I had to defend something that under different circumstances I would criticize.

There was a knock on the bathroom door. Cem poked his head in and looked around carefully. His eyes were large and green, like a deep lake early in the morning. He said he didn't want to come in, because it was the women's bathroom. His voice was shaky. I said I didn't care if he came in or not. He asked if other women were in the bathroom. I said that I cared even less. He came in.

"Come on." Cem said. "Let's go back. There are plenty of other wars on TV." He put his arms around me. "I have an orange. Do you want it? Please stop. Did you know that there are tunnels underneath all of Gaza and that there are more Mercedes than here? Seriously, Gaza will soon get its own Goethestrasse."

I buried my face in his shirt. Cem smelled like good intentions and expensive cologne. He held me tight and whispered, "It's going to be OK. He'll be back soon."

The walls were covered in silk tapestries, white flowers on scarlet red fabric, interwoven with gold strands. I stood in a former brothel in the area close to the central station and looked around. Heavy, artfully cast golden frames decorated the walls, couches and chairs were covered with red velvet. A bartender wore rouge and a tiara, another a nylon stocking on his head. Both served with demonstrative disinterest. Gorgeous girls with shiny mouths and sweet perfume danced to the beat of aggressive house music. The young beauties knew how to accessorize a fetish. Many wore masks and feathers. The men were scantily clad and tried to look like catamites. Everyone smiled, danced, flirted.

I adjusted my dress in front of a mirror. Sami casually leaned on a column. He wore dark jeans and a black leather jacket and was giving the girl next to him a light. The girl was very blond and the contours of her small breasts showed against the thin fabric of her tight dress.

I approached Sami from behind and placed my hand on his broad back. The gesture was both instinctive and surprising, and I stood there with my hand on his back, unsure what to do next. When he turned and smiled at me, I heard myself say, "I didn't know you were in Frankfurt."

The hug was friendly and when we came apart he rested his hand on my arm for a moment. I didn't move until he let go.

"For a month now," said Sami.

"How long are you staying?"

The girl in Sami's company made a show of yawning. I looked at her condescendingly, trying to place all my hatred into this glance, but she ignored me.

"Not longer than necessary," said Sami. "My student visa ran out and I'm waiting for it to get renewed. I'm crashing with my parents and visiting old friends."

Both of us took an awkward sip of our beers. The other girl whispered something into Sami's ear, ran her tongue across her teeth, and finally left.

"Masha, I wanted to call you, but I didn't quite know . . ."

Sami came closer, so that his mouth was close to mine. I stood up on the tips of my toes, stroked his hair out of his face, and kissed his forehead.

"I missed you." Sami breathed into my ear as he had done in the past when we made love. We breathed heavily and almost in the same rhythm. Sami looked like someone who knew exactly what constituted a good life, where to get it, how to hold on to it, and, in the end, how to cast it out before it got too boring. In short: he had the air of something dangerous without being daunting. His gaze was always a little too serious.

I found his nose very erotic. It had a little bump that he'd acquired in a fight in a rural disco that he had started himself.

Even though it had been a long time since we broke up, from time to time I reflexively reached out for him. Sometimes when I felt his body close or when I looked at him for too long, everything was back: love and lust and hunger and greed. Besides, we'd hurt each other so deeply that there was no going back.

In the line in front of the bathroom I spotted Daniel, who looked like a famished, offended rabbit. Daniel called himself anti-German, by which he meant Judeophile, pro-American, and somehow radical left. He was of the type who constantly wanted to save the world through one project or another. First it was nuclear energy, then the rain forest, organic food, and finally the Jews. He especially had a thing for them.

Every time I saw Daniel he laid out his plans—unprompted—for his magnificent future as a gentlemen's tailor in London. Herzl said that if only we wanted to want, it wasn't just a dream, and Daniel wanted and wanted and in the meantime sewed tighter and tighter briefs. I already had three Aperol Spritzes down and tried to avoid him. I looked for Cem, but he was talking on his cellphone in a corner. He was probably talking with his boyfriend, a cook who'd been working in France for three weeks. I didn't understand why Cem was so insistent on attending parties. He hated loud music and people who went to parties. For him, every bash was a battle he fought against himself for every minute he made himself stay.

Daniel had stupidly waved at me. I ignored him, but he started to shout my name across the room, which over time got embarrassing. He made his way toward me hastily, taking large, awkward steps, his hand reaching out for mine, without me extending it. He fidgeted with my sleeve, his breath smelled of beer and bad digestion.

"I'm backing you guys all the way," he said.

"Backing whom?"

"Well, you guys."

Daniel licked his chops and I got angry that he had a clear point of view and all I had was doubts.

"Which you guys?" I was practically yelling, and a few people turned their heads.

"Israel, of course."

"Good save."

"You're mean. So, what do you make of the situation? I mean you, as a Jew."

"Daniel, leave me alone with this crap. What do you want from me? I live in Germany. I have a German passport. I'm not Israel. I don't even live there. I don't vote there and I don't feel any particular connection to the Israeli government."

Daniel always reminded me of my great-aunt, who sat in her Israeli living room—which was an exact replica of her former Soviet living room—drinking tea with a splash of lemon and intently studying *Westi*, the newspaper of the Russian-speaking immigrant population in Israel. *Westi* reported in detail on attacks carried out by Arabs in Israel, desecration of graves carried out by Arabs in France, and everybody's publicly broadcast opinion on Jews.

Daniel thought of Sami as an anti-Semite, Sami thought of Daniel as a Judeophile, and both were right. I would have preferred if they'd not bother me. But during a group project at school Daniel had said that my Arab lover was oppressing me and sucking me dry. An Egyptian plague—those were his words. Thereupon I had hit Daniel and knocked out a tooth and would've been expelled if Daniel hadn't taken all the blame. Of course the blame was his. And not just in a third-generation-since-the-Holocaust kind of way. Ever since his missing tooth he treated me like his personal pet Jew. My only flaw was that I didn't come straight from a German concentration camp.

"I know, I know." Daniel sighed deeply and pulled my sleeve. "The Jews are protected only by governmental force. You know, back in his day, my grandfather was part of a governmental force too, and if your governmental force had existed back then, the whole thing with our governmental force would never have happened. Just because of your collective trauma—" He took a little break. I'd nearly reached the stall, where I could finally lock the door behind me. "I don't want to start a totalitarian discourse with broad abstract terms, don't get me wrong. But it does make sense that many Jews see Israel primarily as a safe haven from genocide. And Auschwitz can happen again anytime. But now you are here, the materialized consequence of the anti-Semitic annihilation fury. Its executive, so to speak. After Auschwitz the Jews have to be able to defend themselves against those who wanted to kill them. My uncle Günther always wanted to kill Jews, but he didn't mean it that way. He didn't fight, he was a paramedic. Nobody from our family actually fought. We're from a small island. There you only fight with the levee. But this . . ."

Daniel took a short deep breath and motioned toward the toilets.

"This is the practical emancipation of the Jews from the permanent threat of destruction. You defend your hard-fought, functioning state with your life. The Israeli army is not an object of discussion, it's not an object at all, but made out of flesh and blood. It's you, your arms and legs, your feet and toes and fingers and hair and night-vision goggles and—"

"Daniel, I am not Israel."

He ran his tongue across his thin lips, looking at me, dumbfounded. "I can't win with you! But you're lucky that I'm well-tempered and go along with everything if I'm into someone." He smiled to himself and sighed. "I'm going to Israel. I booked my ticket today."

"What do you want there?"

He looked at me, shocked, as if he hadn't considered this until now.

"Sunshine."

"What?"

"I spent ten years studying the country. Does that count for nothing?"

The urge to hit him welled up in me again and I had already made a fist when Cem dragged me away. "Come on, let's go. I've had enough. Shit party."

The Main River lay black and calm in front of us. It was almost windless. On the other riverside somebody was fishing in the dark.

"I swear, it was the first porn film we got. In Holland. We'd been looking forward to that vacation for months and the first thing my brother and I did was go into a coffee shop and then search for a porn film. We wanted hard-core and didn't understand a word. We took a tape from the very back, top shelf, of course.

Real hard. And then, finally, we put the tape into the VCR and the only thing we saw was feet. A woman was walking alongside a creek, but we only saw up to her knees. We fast-forwarded, but nothing aside from the feet and the creek. There we were in Holland, liberal country and all; our father had warned us, as had the mullah. We were really horny. And then that. Feet. My brother lost his shit, set the tape on fire and threw it out of the hostel window. He was already doing pretty poorly. Half a year later he died. Did I ever tell you how my brother died? How it took him half a year to kick the bucket?" Cem threw his empty beer bottle into the river and for a moment covered his face with his fingers.

He had told neither Sami nor me how his brother had died. We only knew that it had been a long time ago and that it had been cancer. Often, when Cem was drunk, he cursingly and threateningly promised to tell us how his brother had died. But he never did and we didn't ask, because we, too, had our secrets.

Sami rolled a joint. I reached out for Cem. Cem took my hand and pulled me closer. He said, "Masha, I don't know how to tell you, but all evening I've been getting texts from my cousin telling me not to shop at Aldi over the next few days. Supposedly the profits will go straight to buying arms for the Israeli air force."

"Me too," said Sami.

"You got them too?" Cem asked.

"Yeah. No idea who they're from. I don't even know the numbers."

"And you were afraid of Masha as well?"

"Totally, man. I thought, now she's going to kill me." Sami laughed.

"If you knew what a scene she made today. In the ladies' room."

I placed my head in Sami's lap and Cem leaned over me and said that it's a shame we're no longer together. His best friends.

Sami was hungry, and Cem and I trudged after him. Most shops on the Kaiserstrasse were already closed. A few older women with bleached, stringy hair were still out and about. We passed a twenty-four-hour Laundromat. Inside sat an older couple. Both looked like junkies. He was doing a crossword puzzle, she was clutching a plastic cup, fixated on the swirling laundry with an empty gaze. Their bodies didn't touch.

It had become difficult to go anywhere at night. In the area around the train station everything slowly morphed into grocery stores and fish shops. Granted, it was hard to get cheaper and fresher groceries anywhere, and at noon long lines formed, populated by tired women in tight dresses or ample hijabs, guarded by pimps or other male watchdogs. Sami pulled us into a kebab place and he and Cem ordered. The floor was sticky. A rat skittered across the room. The rotating skewered meat glistened. I ate baklava while everything spun around me. The air was sweet and my body melted into the honey.

8

My head was buzzing. I was lying naked in a dark room.
Behind the bed hung posters of horses and pubescents
who either sang or acted and were shot in similar poses
and colors as the horses. Sami's cellphone was on the
nightstand, my dress hung neatly over the back of a
chair, Sami's shoes stood in front of the chair. He had
always had the habit of tidiness. Even in our relationship everything had been orderly to a fault, but with
time the memories of who had left and humiliated
whom had faded. What remained were the memories
of a few good moments, of a diffuse happiness and of
desire. Back then it had been physical desire, now it was
more the desire to be desired as one had been before.

I quickly got dressed and went into the hallway. In the kitchen, Minna was humming an unfamiliar melody. The air was heavy with the smell of food. It was as if somebody had just deleted the last three years of my life. I saw it all in front of me again. The afternoons shared with Sami, when his little sister never left us alone and Minna constantly told her to do just that. The dinners with Sami's parents, when we spoke a mishmash of French and Arabic, the CDs of Fairuz, that in the morning were accompanied by Minna's song, the feeling of being drunk with love, Sami's touches and the emptiness following the high.

"*Salam alaikum.*" Minna stood in the kitchen door frame and smiled at me. I was happy to see her, even though I would have preferred not to run into her. I wanted to get to the bathroom quickly to wash off last night and Sami.

"*Alaikum salam,*" I greeted Minna.

She gave me a big hug and urged me into the kitchen, where she poured me a flower-decorated mug of Turkish coffee. The breakfast table had already been set.

Minna sat down across from me and curiously examined my face. Her gaze didn't bear the slightest trace of accusation. In the past I had admired her the way you admire other mothers more than your own. When I met her for the first time I swore to become just like her: cheerful and full of warmth. A small Palestinian flag was affixed to the fridge with a black magnet. Minna had been born in a refugee camp in Lebanon.

Sami came out of the bathroom wearing shorts and a worn-out white T-shirt. He didn't look me in the eyes and I glanced away, too. He wore Adilette slippers that were at least two sizes too big for him.

"Habibi, what a sight you are!" Minna said.

Sami gave her a kiss and looked at me, embarrassed.

"Where is Leyla?" I asked.

Leyla was Sami's little sister, and it was her bed I'd woken up in.

"At the Vogelsberg. On a class trip." Sami piled food on his plate that he then didn't touch. Instead he nervously played with his fork. "Abu is at a conference in Switzerland."

"It's a pity he doesn't get to see you. I know he would have loved to. We miss you around here."

"Mom."

I still avoided looking at Sami directly.

"*Kullo min Allah.*" All comes from God. Minna smiled at Sami and me encouragingly, as if to say, It doesn't matter. Nevertheless we both felt uncomfortable. Minna understood, straightened her large body, hugged me, and said, "I hope you'll come back." With these words she left the room.

"*Alors,*" I said and took a bite of the pancake that had been sitting on my plate.

"How are you?" Sami asked after a while.

"Hungover."

Sami stirred his coffee noisily. He stood up, opened the fridge, took out some jam and put it on the table. He stopped behind my chair and massaged my shoulders. I didn't move. Sami kissed the part in my hair, gentle and exploratory. I felt his warm breath on my neck and tightened all my muscles to keep from reacting. His hands left my back and he returned to his seat across from me.

I stayed where I was, paralyzed, unable to say anything. Sami took the jam and looked at the back of the jar, his bushy eyebrows furrowed. He read: " 'Arabic Dream—Peach fruit spread with vanilla and a hint of coffee. Our fruit spreads are made from handpicked fresh fruit from the garden, the local region or mixed orchards.' What are mixed orchards?"

"You don't want to know."

" '. . . which are then turned into exquisite compositions by partially blending them with exotic fruit.' Do you think the exotic fruit are also grown on local mixed orchards? 'A high fruit rate, a pleasant sweetness without artificial additives mark the hand-stirred specialty of our artisanal jam production.' Something is not right about the grammar here."

I wished he would stop reading out loud, but he seemed to enjoy it: " 'Not only breakfast, but many other meals are enriched by fruit spreads. Indulge in the delights of our exquisite compositions.' What the fuck?"

"OK. Let's talk," I said.

"Do you want coffee?" he asked.

"No."

"Sure?"

"Yes."

"I could make some. No trouble at all."

"Sami."

"You could add a spoonful of the Arabic Dream to it."

I stood up. He looked at me. "OK, you want to talk."

Sami jumped up, poured two cups of coffee, full to the brim. Then he started searching through the drawers, turning his back to me.

"What are you looking for?" I asked.

"Sugar," he said.

"I don't take any. As you know."

"But I do."

"You don't take sugar in your coffee."

He turned around briefly and said, "I do." Then he resumed digging through the cupboards.

"No you don't."

"In the States I got into the habit."

"You used to find that disgusting. You can't suddenly like sugar."

"Everything there is way too sweet. Why should coffee be an exception?"

"I can't imagine that Minna wouldn't have any sugar," I said.

"Maybe she used it up, or I can't find it. What do I know?"

"Let's talk."

"Now?"

"Preferably."

"Fuck, I think I have to go to the gas station. We're all out of sugar."

Sami ran out of the kitchen, then I heard the door slam. I raced back into the room, grabbed my things, fell over my own feet, landed flat on the floor in the hallway, and then tried to leave the apartment as quietly as possible. In the stairwell I did my best to avoid another encounter with Sami by climbing up the stairs and waiting one floor up, crouching down while monitoring the staircase. When Sami returned and closed the door behind him, I left my hideout and fled the building.

9

My subway was late. The stream of pedestrians on the opposite track reminded me of a viscous trail of honey, embedded with a few lonely raisins. The woman across from me was wearing a burka. I could only guess her shape. The veil left a thin slit for her eyes. She was following behind a small man who repeatedly turned to her and the child—a chubby-cheeked boy—seated in the stroller she was pushing. The boy clung to a plastic airplane. I leaned on a blue campaign poster for the conservative party: STOP YPSILANTI, AL-WAZIR AND THE COMMUNISTS!

———

When I arrived they were just handing out dinner. A plastic bowl full of brown soup and two slices of wholegrain bread. From the shared bathroom came the sounds of a thundering flush, followed by violent snorts and farts. Elias looked bad: his face was haggard and pale, his eyes red. His hands rested flat on the bed. I asked if he was doing better and he nodded, which again was a lie.

His stubble prickled me as I kissed him. Silently we drank the hospital tea and I climbed into bed next to him and he held me. We had not made love in a long time and now, lying next to him, I remembered the lust and thought that he felt it, too, and I felt guilty. The fall in Minna's apartment had left a big purple bruise on my knee and I hoped that he wouldn't see it. Then I realized that he was crying, without making a sound, just his chest trembling a little. I clung to him tighter, slipped my hands under his pajamas, and kissed him on the mouth. He looked at me apologetically, his eyes full of tenderness and love.

Elias had gotten a new roommate—a small, burly man, artificial hip, Jewish quota–immigrant from Ukraine, presumably demented. He thought Elisha was his grandson Stasik and called for help all night long: "*PO-MOGITE, boze moi, da POMOGITE mne*." HELP, for

God's sake, HELP me. When Elias got up, despite the
pain, and walked over to the man's bed, asking what
was the matter, the man replied: "Stasik, adjust my right
leg. It's hurting so much." Once Elias had finished this
task, hobbled back to his bed, and had almost fallen
asleep again, the screams would start all over. "PO-
MOGITE, boze moi, da POMOGITE mne." Of course
Elias got up again and helped. The procedure went on
like this all night. After two nights and three days Elias
was done with the world. His eyes were bloodshot and
his leg swollen from constantly getting up.

When I visited Elias in the evening, the grandpa
snored complacently. I lay down on the bed next to
Elias. He whispered into my ear, I stroked his arm and
felt his breath. When I traced his breastbone down to
his navel, the neighbor started calling for help again.
I asked him in Russian what was the matter and he
repeated his slogan: "POMOGITE, boze moi, da PO-
MOGITE mne." I rang the bell for the nurse. She came
right away and asked him, also in Russian, what was
the matter. When she didn't get a reply, she waited for a
moment and then repeated her question. This time, the
man answered, as if under torture, "Water."

She gave him water, spoke a few encouraging words,
and he said: "POMOGITE, boze moi, da POMOGITE
mne." Whereupon she shrugged, shot us an apologetic
look, and left.

"I would love to travel with you once I'm out of here," said Elias.

"Where should we go?"

"Where would you like? Tel Aviv?"

"*POMOGI, Stasik, POMOGI.*"

I went over to him and again asked what was wrong. He called me Stasik as well and asked me for water. I gave him his sippy cup but he changed his mind and asked me to adjust his pillow. I adjusted his pillow, but then he wanted me to move his left leg, and when I did it, I saw that he grinned. The grandpa grinned.

It was time to take action against the grandpa. The next day I skipped my seminar on French engineering terminology and went to the hospital early in the afternoon. The grandpa's daughter stood at the entrance of the ward. She was shrouded in a cloud of Chanel and cigarette smoke. I had seen her once, briefly, in Elias's room. Next to her was a frail old lady with noticeably expensive jewelry and purple hair, accompanied by a nurse.

When I greeted them they paid no attention to me. Nevertheless I joined their group. The old lady lamented heartrendingly in Yiddish. About her fate. Her husband's fate, her cat, the hospital, the hospital sheets. I took a deep breath and introduced myself. Then I said that something had to be done regarding her father and husband, respectively. They said nothing and stared at me. They stared at my dirty white sneakers and my tattered jeans.

The younger one stubbed out her cigarette and started speaking loudly and quickly: her father had been a partisan, fighting against the Germans in the Ukrainian forests. Was it too much to ask to take care of a veteran, or was my husband a Nazi? Or maybe he wasn't even my husband? Maybe that was the reason why he hadn't married me yet? If I had the irrepressible urge to complain about an honorable man, I should talk to his nurse, Bella. Thereupon the daughter left. Her perfume remained.

Bella grinned. She wore brown leather shoes and a beige suit. A butch through and through.

The yellow eyes of the old lady glowed maliciously. The diamonds sparkled in her old ears. She, too, berated me. We should be ashamed of ourselves, unmarried, fucking in her husband's room as if it were nothing. She actually said *fucking*. I blushed and wanted to reply something, but the nurse laughed, shot her a stern look as if she was her property, and whispered to me: "No worries, she's a slut herself. I had to take her to the gynecologist countless times. And the things he excavated from her—rags, bottles. For her, only size matters."

Suddenly the old lady started yelling at me: What kind of a woman was I? How dare I talk to her, the wife of a partisan? My husband must have ordered me from a Ukrainian catalog. Did I have no manners at all?

I left both of them alone.

10

This afternoon Elias was to be released from the hospital. I had spent half the morning painstakingly waxing hair from my body. Then I cleaned, swept, mopped, and went shopping.

At the entrance to the supermarket I took a basket in due form. Then I stood around indecisively in the vegetable section before finally moving to the aisles, where I started filling my basket with random items. I would squeeze oranges, caramelize pears, cut and steam vegetables, stay clear of the pork, knead dough, then roll out and bake it. I just didn't know how to do all this and therefore added a few housewifey magazines to my shopping basket. Another woman also stood indecisively in the aisles. She had soft features, wore no makeup, and had on flat gray velvet shoes with a little bow on each rounded toe. She studied the small print on the boxes, wheezed, then lunged at a super-market employee, waving her tote bag threateningly. "That's just not possible. The organic lettuce can't be sold out. Just like that? You're hiding it. The other one is no good, you understand me? No good. All that stuff comes from America!" And then she broke out in tears. The undercover security guard and I looked at her, stunned.

At the cash register I got a pack of cigarettes and smiled. My fingers drummed a march on the conveyor belt. The female neck on line in front of me was so per-fect, so slender and white, that it immediately sparked a desire in me.

Elias filled the bed again. I was grateful that he lay there, on his back, his arms spread wide, breath-ing calmly and regularly. The comforter wasn't big enough to cover his feet, arms, and shoulders at the same time. So I covered him with my half and went into the kitchen to get a glass of water and cigarettes. Then I sat down on the windowsill. The bedroom seemed somehow bigger now, and the sticky, grayish layer of dust that covered the white wood of the shelves now rested in the dark—colorless like everything else. The morning air was fresh. I stubbed out my cigarette and crawled back into bed. In his sleep Elisha turned to me and kissed my shoulder and continued sleeping peacefully.

His absence had come as a shock. It was almost like back when Sibel left. The apartment had been too full of emptiness. Elias hadn't been there to eat, to sweat, to sleep, to breathe, or to look at me. Everything in our apartment belonged to him. Most of the furniture, the kitchen, the table, the bookshelves. Elias had built our bed himself.

She said she was from northern Germany. She said Rügen, but I didn't believe her. Her family was Turkish, and very traditional. Three older brothers—all born in Germany, equipped with an old-fashioned sense of honor. Sibel wasn't allowed to have boyfriends or talk with Germans, Yugoslavians, or Russians. She wasn't allowed to leave the house after dark. One of her brothers accompanied her to school. When he decided that Sibel had looked at her teacher a little too long he branded her back with a flatiron. Sibel's father was appalled, he walked in circles on the living room carpet and then beat Sibel's brother. Then he drank some tea and slapped Sibel's mother in the face, because the tea had cooled too quickly and because she allowed her daughter to dress like a German. Sibel was pulled out of school and her father started researching in an Internet cafe for a husband. Sibel's father was determined to get a good deal. Even if Sibel wouldn't get a big dowry, she was a German citizen and therefore attractive to many. Marriage was the only legal way to get into Europe and Europe was the big hope.

Sibel refused the first potential husband and the second as well, and for that she got a beating from her oldest brother. The youngest, a year older than she, held her, slipped his hand in her panties and whispered into her ear: "You are a disgrace to our family. We will kill you." Her mother said: "He is a good man. He will work for you, protect you. Do you think anybody will fall in love with you, just because you are young and pretty? That he'll stay with you forever? That he'll love you? Don't be so naive. Please don't be so naive." Sibel stood facing a mirror and cried because she was naive. Wanted to be.

Sibel ran away and at first stayed with a German friend. But her friend's parents were afraid of Muslim men, without even needing to be told about Sibel's own experience with Muslim men. Or about Islam. After three days Sibel was back out on the street. Bitter and alone.

She only wore dresses, skirts, silk blouses, and shoes with shiny buckles. She walked on tiny, clattering heels and looked like candy. Innocent, irresistible, and absolute. Twice she fucked my lovers. I had hated her for it, in a Germanly thorough fashion. But I couldn't stop desiring her. The apartment and landline were in my name. I did money transfers for her and when she had to go to the doctor she borrowed my insurance card.

She slept without a cover. Her underwear shimmered dusky pink. No, she only pretended to be asleep. For a long time I looked at her skinny body, the bent knees and the straight dark hair that spilled across her pillow. The curtains were drawn and the room was bathed in a soft light. We'd had a week of beautiful weather. Nothing in the sky moved. The closest thing to a cloud was the occasional vapor trail from a plane. Sibel breathed calmly and regularly, didn't hear the buzz of the houseflies. I pulled my dress over my head. In the window across the street the curtain moved. I unhooked my bra, took off my panties, and sat down on the bed. I leaned over her and kissed her shoulder. She smiled without opening her eyes. I traced her areolas with my fingers.

"You dirty little thing," she whispered into my ear and laughed. "Did you know that Kurdish girls always kiss each other on the mouth, as a substitute for real sex? They can't afford riding lessons."

"Are you a Kurd, Sibel?"

She looked at me, grinned, but didn't answer. Then she turned over onto her stomach. Her entire body was covered with scars.

The calls had started when we made love almost every night, first in the middle of the night, then on late mornings, then during the day. The caller didn't say anything. We heard nothing but his heavy breathing. Sibel started leaving the lights on in the hallway at night and didn't leave the house by herself anymore. She took taxis, even if her trip would only take her five minutes on foot.

One evening the entire apartment went dark. At the same moment, Sibel's cellphone rang. The number was blocked. On the other end, somebody breathed heavily and remained silent.

"My brother works for the secret service!" Sibel yelled, as I fumbled with the fuse box. I was almost as scared as she was, if for different reasons.

When I came home from school the next day, Sibel was gone. She had taken with her her shimmery dresses, hair clips, cosmetics, and perfume samples, as well as my passport, my insurance card, and cash.

11

I met with Sami in a small cider bar that smelled of beer and frying oil. Nonetheless it seemed to be very popular with the local alcoholics and tourists. We sat at the last free table, right by the swinging door that led to the kitchen and the bathrooms. The regulars wore sweatpants and sweatshirts. A group of Irish tourists provided some variety, commenting loudly on their hotel and World War II. Older gentlemen with reddish faces and good spirits. I forgot who had suggested this as a meeting place, Sami or me. At least we wouldn't run into anyone we knew.

Two waitresses lingered behind the bar, giggling. The older one sported a leathery tan and blue eyeliner.

The younger looked like she still stood a chance. Although the bar was packed, they didn't have a lot to do. The guests didn't order much. The younger one glanced at Sami and approached our table.

Earlier, Elias had sat on the sofa while I got ready. I'd put on a tight dress, rouge, and a bit of perfume behind the ears. All for another guy. Where was I going? he'd asked. I'm meeting Sami, I'd answered, and tried to hide my nervousness. But Elias understood anyway. Angrily remained silent. He had used up all his energy on the fifteen steps it took him to get from our bedroom to the living room.

Now, sitting across from Sami, I remained quiet, still feeling Elias's eyes on me. A cross adorned with rhinestones dangled over the waitress's generous cleavage. Both of us ordered cider, although neither of us liked it.

"My visa application was rejected," Sami said. Deep shadows hung under his eyes. He sat across from me with hanging shoulders and held my hands in his.

"Again?"

The waitress placed the two ciders in front of us and smiled at Sami, but he ignored her flirtation. The glasses were scratched. Sami had been my first boyfriend. Before him, love had always ended in rejection.

"Now what?" I said.

"I'll definitely lose this semester. I just hope it won't be an entire year. I don't want to be thrown out of the Ph.D. program." His voice sounded tired and uncertain. In the past he'd been the stronger one, always busy and determined. The one who blazed his trail undeterred.

I wanted to say something encouraging, anything that would wipe away his resigned expression. "Do you think they'd throw you out?" I asked instead and bit my lip.

He gave a little laugh: "It would be a miracle if they didn't."

Sami clinked his glass with mine and drank. I had expected that the meeting would be strange, or at least awkward, but everything felt natural. I stroked Sami's cheek. He turned my hand over and pulled it closer to his nose.

"You smell good."

"I smell like I always do."

"That's what I mean."

I pulled my hand back, shifting nervously on my chair.

Sami put his hands on the table, looked at them, and said: "I can't sleep. I drift off, but in the middle of the night I get up again. Wide awake. I lie on the couch in my parents' living room and can't figure things out. I don't know what to do with myself. I pace the apartment, read magazines and novels. Mostly Russian ones." Sami paused and looked me directly in the eyes. I didn't avoid his gaze.

"My apartment in the States is empty. My sister is sleeping in my old childhood room. I'm neither here nor there. If I knew at least how long I have to stay, I would get a room. Do something. Not vegetate in constant transit."

"And during the day? What do you do then?"

"I try to make progress on my research. But that's ridiculous. In the morning I go to the library and read. But by noon I'm tired already. I'm always tired, but I stay in the library, not wanting to go home. Most of all I don't want Minna to see me like this." He paused, emptied his glass in one gulp, and ordered a new one. "She asks about you all the time."

Our feet touched under the table. The English conversation grew louder, but I couldn't discern distinct words from the babble of voices. They played a drinking game and sang a song. The waitress brought them round after round of shots.

I looked at Sami, felt a warmth inside me and a longing for Elias. His touch, his bad mood, his smell.

"I don't want to get home too late," I said. Sami nodded and signaled the waitress.

The night was starlit. In silence we walked to the tram stop. I shivered. Sami waited with me for my tram, which I interpreted as a fond gesture. When the tram pulled up he gave me a kiss on the cheek and waited until I'd made it through the doors. A light rain set in.

It was already dark in the apartment, although it wasn't even eleven. Rain dripped from my umbrella onto the linoleum floor and—good girl that I was—I opened it and set it down to dry. The distant rumble of the tram and the weak glow of streetlamps trickled into our apartment from outside. I opened the fridge. The upper shelf was full of Elias's film. I angled in the freezer for the vodka bottle and poured myself a glass. All without turning on the light. The alcohol burned in my throat and warmed me. Then I quickly took off all my clothes and stepped into the shower. It took a little while to wash away the smell of the bar and the thoughts of Sami.

Elias lay on my side of the bed, the cover pulled over his face. I inched my way forward. He took me into his arms and gave me a strong hug, and I hugged him back just as strongly. Affirming for him and for me. We stayed like that, breathing in the breath of the other, and didn't dare to move.

"What time is it?" Elias murmured.

"Eleven."

"Good. You came home early." He fell asleep. I lay next to him, awake, and was suddenly afraid, but didn't know of what.

In the morning we made love to the sound of yelling drunkards, ignoring their screams with aristocratic calm. Afterward we lay next to each other for a long time. Elias stroked my hip and kissed my back until he sat up and said, "I've lost a lot of weight, haven't I?"

I also sat up and took him in.

"It's because I only lie down these days." He quietly added, "All my muscles are gone."

I placed my right palm on his face, kissed the tip of his nose, and said, "They'll come back. Everything is going to be fine." And because he looked at me skeptically I added, "I promise."

He smiled and I suggested, "I'll make us breakfast, OK?"

"We've got to do something to put some meat back on my bones, right?"

"Exactly. Because I never ever want to go back to that hospital," I said.

Elias started asking his questions again. We lay in bed, body to body. The rain pounded against the window. We'd just had our first nice evening together in ages. No fighting, just pizza and a movie, without any trace of anger.

We fought over every little thing. He didn't recover, the pain was bad, and he could hardly move.

For the first few weeks after the surgery he couldn't put his full weight on his leg, which meant he couldn't get up without help. I went to the supermarket, to the bakery, to the dry cleaner. I hung laundry, washed dishes, vacuumed, cooked, went to the library. In the evening I felt drained, fell into bed, and went to sleep right away. Elias would lie awake next to me for a long time, only beginning to drift off with the first rays of morning light. He didn't like my cooking, pushed food around his plate, didn't eat. An hour later, he would put a pot of milk on the stove. And then, with a grave expression, he would dip Nutella sandwiches into the pot. I didn't say anything, but treated him coolly. I knew that it was childish, but I was over-worked and overwrought. Elias increasingly accused me of being distant.

But despite our tense mood, we mostly managed to hold back. Sometimes he did well and then friends would come over to watch movies and drink beer. But those days were rare.

"What happened back then in Baku?" He posed the question quickly and out of the blue.

I held my breath, thought for a while, then said, "I've told you already."

Elias struggled to sit up.

"You have to start trusting me," he said.

"It's not about that." My voice sounded harsh.

"What's it about then?"

I sat up too, and turned on the bedside light.

"What's up with your father?" I asked.

His expression became even more tense.

"What do you mean?" he asked hesitantly.

"Did he ever beat you?"

Elias stared at me, shocked by the turn our conversation had just taken. "What do you mean?" he asked again.

"When he was drunk, did he beat you?" My voice broke. Remorse crept in.

"Sometimes he drank for days on end, and then for months he didn't touch a sip. It was a toss-up. I never knew what state he would be in. Mostly he drank at night, when my mother was at work. I brought him to bed and cleared away the bottles and vomit before my mother came home in the morning.

"She left you alone with him?"

"What choice did she have? She worked, put up with his moods and self-importance without saying a word. Right after the Wall came down he lost his job. But he'd started drinking long before that. Well, what do I know?" Elias fell silent. I waited, although I knew that he wouldn't say anything more. But after a while he continued and I asked myself what I knew about Elias and if I really knew him at all.

"On the days when he couldn't speak in coherent sentences anymore, I would sometimes take pictures of him. One day he found the box with the photographs."

"And then?"

Elias turned off the light and buried his face in the cushion. I reached underneath his T-shirt and stroked his back and covered his neck with kisses. But he didn't move. Still, in the following days Elias would tell me even more. It was as if a dam had burst inside him.

12

When I was a child I often went for walks to the park with my mother. In the afternoon, and sometimes in the mornings, too. In the park there were rides, *katcheli*, that were all broken. Or they lacked the electricity to get them going. Mother often told me scary stories about the *Katchelchik*.

My favorite game at the time was News, and it went sort of like this: Divide up the park and try to take over the others' territories. By any means necessary. Just like on the news that aired on TV after the cartoons. We played National Front. We played war.

I don't remember his name, but the boy had red hair. Even his feet and knees were covered in freckles.

He was my enemy. My personal Nagorno-Karabakh. We fought. One of us always cried. Which probably was because we battered each other with sticks and stones. And then the boy entrenched himself in a tree. It was a large, beautiful tree at the edge of the park, far away from our mothers. From a high branch he threw stones and nails, and when I'd almost conquered the tree—just as the Armenian forces had done with Shusha—our mothers decided we should reconcile. The redheaded boy's father was the chief of police and had excellent access to the black market. The enemy's mother was a small woman with long red hair. In the park she always bragged about marital love—every day her husband returned home during his lunch break to make fervent love to her. She confuses sex with love, I heard my mother say—not without a trace of jealousy in her voice.

The mothers negotiated in the kitchen. My enemy and I stood in the parents' bedroom, in front of the mirror of a large wardrobe. He chose a silken dress and I a white dress shirt. Above our heads hung a framed photograph of Saddam Hussein. The enemy assumed a Napoleonic pose and quoted his father. Said that Saddam was a real man. The only real man far and wide. Except for his dad, of course. Saddam's dad? The redhead thought for a moment. No, his own father. Saddam is also the only one who can contend with the

Jews. When I told him that I was a Jew, too, he wasn't surprised.

Only a few weeks later he and his mother had to flee. The husband had told his wife that he could no longer guarantee her safety, nor the safety of their children. They had to leave the city immediately. He stayed in the apartment, even though it belonged to his Armenian father-in-law.

My mother tried to save a few things from the apartment, to send them to the woman who was now in hiding. His new wife had already moved in. An Azeri woman. While my mother packed up books and sheet music, the woman didn't protest. She only cast around contemptuous glances, as if she was the one who was being robbed. When my mother started packing up the silverware that had been part of the dowry alongside the apartment, the new one perched her hands on her hips and threatened, "That you'll leave here. Or else I call for my husband."

The most difficult thing was to get home with the suitcase. Everyone carrying a suitcase was taken for an Armenian by the angry mob and instantly lynched. My father hid in the next driveway with the suitcase, while my mother stood at the entrance to the driveway and waited for a group of *pogromchiki* to pass by. Only then would he leave and run to the next driveway.

Elias was busy with the pots. I approached from behind, put my arms around his waist, and leaned onto his back. He didn't turn around and I let go.

"Elias?"

He remained standing with his back to me. I put my hand on his shoulder, but he shook it off. For a while I studied his back, then I sat down at the table.

"What's the matter?"

"Nothing."

He turned around. His nose was red and his eyes were shiny. Then he asked unflinchingly: "Is anything going on between you and Sami?"

I took a plate from the table, smashed it against the wall with full force and only missed his head by a little.

I saw the uncertainty well up in his eyes and yelled: "Do you think I fuck him while you're in the hospital?"

He shook his head.

"How'd you get that idea in the first place?" I asked.

"All this lying around is driving me crazy."

"You're full of shit." My hands shook and I continued yelling: "Everyone loves within their limits. If that's not enough for you . . ."

Elias looked at me, distressed, and I knew that I had gone too far. Now the ease between us was over. I turned to face the window and opened it. Tears filled my eyes. I shouldn't have said anything. I had never before threatened Elias. Never exerted power and had hoped that we would never reach this point in our relationship. But now we had, and I was to blame. I heard Elias try to bend over to pick up the shards.

"Stop it!" I said.

"I'll take care of it," Elias murmured, and I couldn't bear his pitiful glance.

"I said stop it."

"No, I'll take care of it."

"But you can't."

Elias put the gathered shards on the table and hobbled into the bedroom. When he tried to open the door, he slipped. His body hit the floor with a dull thud. I ran over, tried to help him up, but he pushed me away.

13

I turned on the light. Elias sat upright against the head-board. His breath was labored, his hair drenched with sweat. All of a sudden I was wide awake.

"What's going on?"

"Cramps," he said.

"In your leg?"

"Yes."

He shivered. Arms, legs, hands. The teeth, too, chattered. Pearls of sweat gathered on his upper lip. I opened the bandage. The leg didn't look noticeably swollen, but the wound was red around the edges and pus-filled in the center.

"I'm calling an ambulance."

"No."

"No?"

"I don't want to go back to the hospital. Let's wait until tomorrow."

"No."

"It's only cramps. That happens. Tomorrow we'll go back. I'm sure they couldn't do much in the ER now anyway. I might just as well stay here. Get me some water, please."

I went into the kitchen and filled a glass with water. Up to the brim. Then I washed my hands, took two clean towels and poured cold water over one and boiling hot water over the other. Back in the bedroom, I tried to appear calm, to smile at Elias, but I didn't succeed. I placed the cold compress on Elias's forehead, and then with the disinfected towel went on to dab the pus from the wound. As soon as I touched the wound Elias screamed, jerked up, back bent, and then fell back with a groan. I dialed the number for the ambulance and wiped Elias's face with the wet towel. The windows of the house across the street slowly lit up, one by one.

His entire body was shivering. I tried holding on to him, hugged him, but one cramp chased the other in increasingly short intervals. The wound dripped. I lay down next to him. Elias hit the headboard full force, cursed and whimpered. An eternity passed before I heard the siren in front of our house. From the window I yelled down the floor number and begged them to hurry up. Finally I heard the heavy steps of the emergency doctor and the paramedic on the stairs. I led them into the bedroom, where Elias was writhing in the sheets. I rattled off Elias's medical history. The doctor nodded and put on white rubber gloves.

"Calm down," he said to me while taking Elias's pulse and patting down the wound. Elias screamed in agony. I tried to soothe him, put my hand in his. Nothing worked. The doctor took a syringe from his case and gave Elias the injection. Then he continued the examination. He studied the wound pensively and started patting it again.

Elias broke out in a cold sweat. "Stop!" he yelled. His hand clawed into mine and he turned his head away. At first I assumed he didn't want to watch, but it turned out to be a cramp in his neck. For a couple of minutes, Elias convulsed in pain, hardly able to breathe.

"How long has there been pus in the wound?" the physician asked.

"Maybe a couple of hours. I don't know. I slept through it. Can't you give him something?"

"I already did."

When the seizure ended, the doctor gave the paramedic a signal. Without a word the paramedic went down to the ambulance and a few minutes later came back with another colleague and a stretcher. Elias had calmed down a bit. His groans were quieter and he could breathe again. The neighbors peered out of their windows curiously.

As soon as we arrived at the hospital a nurse asked me when Elias had last eaten.

part two

1

I knew it as soon I saw the doctor approaching. He was tired and pale and took me by the elbow and guided me into a separate room, where he had me sit down on an examination table. I only understood bits and pieces: emergency surgery, complications, outflow of bone marrow, complications, fat embolism, not rare, complications, drop in blood pressure, cardiac arrhythmia, cardiac arrest.

He took off his glasses and wiped his forehead.

"He couldn't be revived. Do you want to see his body?"

Elisha lay on the bed. His body was cold, but not yet stiff. His eyes were shut. They had dressed him in a hospital gown. I opened it. The surgery wound on his thigh had been carelessly stitched. His chest had been closed in the same coarse fashion. I sat down on the edge of the bed. A nurse opened the door a crack, apologized, and came in. I waited until she had left, then locked the door. He couldn't die. Only a few meters away. He should have waited for me. We could have died together. I wouldn't have minded. I sang nursery rhymes for him, as if I wanted to cradle him to sleep. I sang badly and hoped something would move in his face, a brief twitch at the corners of his mouth, a flared nostril, a blink, a flick of his hand, but I knew that he was dead. With the nail of my index finger I traced his skin, at first with more pressure, then softly. He was motionless, cold. A ray of light divided the room in two halves. I lay down next to him on the bed as his body became increasingly stiff. There was no glowing sunrise. The sky was completely white. Elisha had always said that such light meant it was going to be a hot day. Somebody knocked. Morning came and the knocking became a hammering.

According to Jewish faith the soul leaves the body at the time of death, but sticks around nearby until the body has been buried. Therefore the body must not be left alone. But Elisha wasn't Jewish, and I wasn't religious. Somebody yelled my name. At some point the nurse and two doctors, whom I didn't know, were standing in front of me. I hadn't even heard them unlock the door. One of them had a broad back and a weathered face and reminded me of the Russian swimmer Alexander Popov. I'd been sitting next to my mother in front of the TV when Popov won gold at the Olympics in Barcelona. The doctor pushed me into a chair.

I left the hospital, crossed the narrow street, and waited at the bus stop. Birds were chirping and the bus was on time. The bus driver said hello and I sat down in the last row and pressed my face against the scratched window. The landscape was still there. Long rows of parked cars, small houses, well-tended gardens. Here and there a tree.

I got off at the first subway stop. Went down, threw the trash from my pockets into an overflowing bin that was swarming with flies. I threw up. I wiped my mouth. A few punks took a piss onto the tracks and laughed. The subway came and the punks lifted their backpacks and got on, one after the other. The air in the car was stuffy. The stops cycled in and out, and along with them the passengers, most of whom had their backs turned to me. I was in front of my door and then in the hallway of the apartment. I hung my keys on the hook next to the door and took off my shoes.

In the bathroom I was hit by a wall of warm, moist air. The water was scalding hot. The drain cover was full of blond hair. His hair. There were unopened letters on the kitchen table that were addressed to Elisha. Under the pillow was his T-shirt. There was a smell of his sweat and of milk in the air, although Elisha had very rarely smelled sweaty and never smelled like milk. After a while, only the scent of sour milk would remain. I coiled up and everything around me began to spin. I could feel the sickness rising. I staggered into the bathroom and threw up next to the toilet. My circulatory system, my knees and palms, all signaled that my body was throwing in the towel. I trembled and lay back down in bed, and nothing seemed more urgent to me than sleeping.

2

My mother took care of everything. She took care of Horst and Elke, the phone, the formalities and the rest. She lit a candle next to Elisha's photo and covered the mirrors. I lay in bed, didn't change my clothes, and stared at the ceiling. Sometimes Mother came in, sat down next to me, and emptied out the bucket next to the bed. Since I couldn't eat, I only threw up bile.

The Talmud demands that one remember the dead. If I'd had it on hand I would have thrown it into a fireplace. But it was in some box next to a *Schindler's List* videotape. I wanted to remember everything. His face and his body. Under no circumstances did I want to forget how he held me in his arms, how his lips felt on my skin, how he smiled and how we fell asleep next to each other. How we talked on the phone in the evening when we were apart. Forgetting became my biggest fear. I lay in bed, the curtains drawn, and on the nightstand there was the lit candle in front of his photo. If I closed my eyes I saw his face and if I kept them closed for too long I saw the face of a young corpse in a light blue gown. Her cavernous eyes, blood dripping from her abdomen. Before the images could merge, I blinked and took a sip of water. Then I could see Elias again. I remembered the way my body fit perfectly into his. I thought of his voice, his hands, and how I had found him in a small, smoky apartment.

The Croatian hosts had slowly bobbed their heads in sync with the Slavic hip-hop. I had a cigarette and a glass of vodka in hand and combed through the rooms searching for people I knew. A recent high school graduate pulled me into the kitchen, wanted me to touch his biceps. The food spoke of the hosts' loyalty to the Balkan snack bar owned by their aunt. The living room was bursting with people. Elias sat on the sofa, flirting aggressively with Tuba. He had a girly face with sunken cheeks and high cheekbones. Dimples formed at the edges of his smile. A harmless-little-boy haircut. His clear, even skin and a delicate net of freckles around his finely cut nose completed the picture. I liked tall, slender men and faces dominated by noses, and had spent far too long watching him already.

Tuba brushed her hair out of her face, bracelets rattling, and took another swig from the beer bottle. In the process, she stuck out her tongue a little and briefly licked the bottleneck. Suddenly she waved.

"Masha!"

I slowly wove my way through the dancing crowd. Somebody spilled beer on my shoe and apologized with a nod.

"Sweetheart, how are you? This is Elias." Tuba looked at me and Elias, alternatingly, and played with her hair—seemingly lost in thought. She twirled a strand of hair around her index finger, tightened it, and let it bounce again. Then she asked me, "Are you here with Cem?"

"Yes, but I haven't seen him in an hour."

"I'll go look for him." Tuba disappeared. I sat down next to Elias and sat up straight. The situation was a little awkward for both of us. At first we just sat there in silence. Then I asked him where he was from. He spoke of Dresden, Hamburg, and Berlin, of fishing and architecture, of French films, the new exhibition at the modern art museum, of soccer and the mole behind my left ear.

We left the party together. It was drizzling and Elias asked me whether he could give me a ride home on his bike. He studied me so intensely and seriously, as if he wanted to learn me by heart. I took the night bus. As I was regretting my decision in solitude at the bus stop, it began to hail.

Three weeks later I ran into Elias on the tram. Next to us stood a boy with a transparent bag in his hand. In the bag swam a goldfish. Elias and I looked at the boy, puzzled, but he paid no attention to us. I wanted to slip Elias my number, but he got off too soon.

Over the next weeks I constantly thought of him. Then I read in the newspaper about an exhibition in the Staedel school. I even bought a new dress, but it was too cold to take off my coat. Elias stood in the corner, leaning on the bar, cigarette hanging from the corner of his mouth. Next to him was a girl. Red short skirt, coralline lips. A pretty girl, with immaculate skin and immaculate legs. When I saw her, I knew I had no choice but to accept our German girl and her immaculate legs. I stormed out. He caught me at the entrance, by the sleeve. We went back in. He bought me a beer and I was afraid of saying something stupid. And then he said the only thing that most pictures need to become art is empty walls. I grew increasingly nervous. I liked his nose and wasn't thinking anymore about Sami, who had returned to California a couple of months ago.

The ash of my cigarette left burn marks on the sheet. I lay in the half-empty bed and saw the corpse of the young woman in the blue gown hit the pavement directly in front of my feet. Eyes rolled up, bleeding abdomen. I freed myself from my father's grip and ran over to the woman. Her dress was soaked with blood that pooled around her on the asphalt and ran up to my shoes. Dyed them red.

My mother greeted Cem with overwhelming geniality and made him coffee.

Cem sat down at my bedside and said that he and his friend had hired professional mourners in Greece for Elias, who during the next forty-eight hours would wail over Elias's death. I could watch them over a live stream on the Internet. He had set up a YouTube channel specifically for that purpose. He pulled a laptop from his bag and on the screen I saw two veiled old women who did nothing but sit on two white plastic garden chairs in an almost empty room. Cem stared at the screen disappointedly and cursed in Turkish. Then he called Konstantin, whom I heard cursing on the other end of the line as well. Konstantin in turn must have called somebody in Greece, as a mere fifteen minutes later the professional mourners got to work:

they screamed, wailed, and sobbed. We watched them for a while and they kept repeating one sentence over and over. At least it sounded like one sentence to us. I asked Cem what it meant but he didn't know. We called Konstantin again.

"I can't hear it," said Konstantin. "It's too quiet."

We held the phone closer to the screen.

"Wisdom cometh by suffering," translated Konstantin.

"Why are they quoting from the *Oresteia*?" Cem asked.

"They are Greeks," said Konstantin.

"Call them again," said Cem.

I lay alone in the double bed, running my hands over the empty half of the bed and trying to find a different sleeping position from my usual one. My thoughts kept returning to his last night. I examined every second, certain that I could've averted his death if only I'd woken up earlier. I should have taken a look at the wound the day before. I felt responsible for Elias's death. Most nights I fell into a restless sleep in the early morning hours and then delayed getting up. I imagined Elisha lying next to me. I would reach out for him and he would be there, lying on his side of the bed, with bent knees and disheveled hair. I would lean over him and wish him a good morning. His stubble would be scratchy. I would touch him. His body would be warm. I would hold on to him and never want to let go. Then he would push me aside, get up, go to the bathroom, come back, and maybe briefly snuggle up again. He would wear clothes that didn't match. I would make fun of him for it. The sheets still had a faint smell of him and I wore his clothes to sleep. It was only when the morning came that I would look for him in the bed and remember.

3

Before turning the key in the ignition my father silently
folded his hands for a moment over the steering wheel.
Not in prayer, but in accordance with a Russian tradition
that all travel should begin with silence and in a seated
position. After the silence he pulled out and began ac-
celerating immediately, even though we were still in the
residential area. The pine-scented air freshener swung
wildly from the rearview mirror. Mother smiled con-
tently and sank deeper into her seat. I sat in the back,
between Cem and Sami, both of whom were asleep.

Sami's student visa for the United States had ex-
pired. Normally something like this took two weeks,
but if the passport lists an Arabic name and Beirut as

the place of birth, even German citizenship was of little help. Once a month Sami went to the U.S. consulate, filled out forms, and was assured that it wouldn't take much longer, just a few weeks, a routine check. This is what he was told, every month, for almost a year.

The glowing red of morning hung heavy in the sky. As my father drove his Volkswagen insistently in the left lane and well beyond the speed limit, giving way to neither BMWs nor Mercedes, my mother looked at him tenderly. Sometimes I asked myself what our life would have looked like if my father had made it into space. I asked myself if he would have been happy then. If my mother would have been happier. Most likely it would have been enough if we had stayed in the Caucasus. Or if I had been a better daughter.

Horst and Elke lived in a peach-colored house in the Mediterranean prefab style that looked a little lost in the eastern German province. An oak tree growing next to a white front door. The curtains drawn. Meticulously cut lawn. Toolshed. Behind their house the village ended.

As we pulled up, they came to the front door, both wearing black. When we got out of the car the doors shut noisily and Elke winced.

My mother hugged Elias's mother, careful to keep their bodies from getting too close. Father shook Horst's hand, as firmly as he could. Cem and Sami also offered their condolences. In the hallway, Horst took our coats and passed them off to Elke. Having dealt with the coats, Elke ran her palms over her thighs. Her satin pants were a little on the tight side. She smiled nervously, brushing the hair out of her face. Mother grinned, feeling superior, and pushed her purse into my dad's hands. She wore a black dress that showed off her underweight figure, high heels, and a pearl necklace from my great-grandmother's prerevolutionary times.

Cem and Sami, embarrassed, took off their shoes. Elke started asking questions. Whether we had found the way easily, how the drive had been, when we'd left, if it hadn't been too strenuous a drive. The questions came at a machine gun pace, but no one answered. Horst pointed at a brown leather couch. Seven coffee cups and pieces of cake had been placed on the coffee table. The room was a perfect German Democratic Republic still life.

"That's from the bakery. Right around the corner." Horst's voice trembled. He jerked up and closed the window, blocking out all sounds from outside—chirping birds and children laughing in the distance.

After a while, when nobody could bear the silence any longer, Cem asked, "Do you collect clocks?"

On the opposite wall hung dozens of clocks, carved from wood and painted. Their collective ticking amounted to a nerve-wracking clatter.

"No," said Horst, the alcoholic.

"I see," Cem nodded.

Sami choked on the cake and my father patted him on the back.

"You've got quite a few, though."

Elke placed her chubby hand on Horst's knee and smiled at us. "They were my father's."

"Did he collect clocks?"

"Yes."

Horst cleared his throat and asked me, "Did you bring his things?"

"Since you may not have the space for them," Elke said in a soft voice. She ran her hands over her pants and looked past me.

"But it's your decision." Horst went over to the window again.

"She doesn't want to." My father looked from one to the other. In his eyes, I could see he was ready for a fight, if needed.

My mother hastened to praise the cake, Elke hastened to offer more coffee.

My father said, this time with more emphasis, "If she doesn't want to, she doesn't want to." His German always came out sounding a little rude. In Russian he was more diplomatic. His posture was different when he spoke German: straight back, muscles flexed. His German remained basic, accompanied by a Turkish sound, Russian syntax, and Latin foreign words.

Cem passed the sugar bowl to my father and resumed the conversation: "How many clocks do you
have?"

"I don't know. Strange that you should ask," said
Elke.

"Thirty-six," Horst replied peevishly.

"*Çüş*," commented Cem.

"Really? That many? I would never have guessed."
Elke smiled shyly and topped off everyone's coffee.
"Yes, it is exhausting. They always have to be wound
up. That takes time."

"And the noise doesn't bother you?"

"The noise?"

"Well, the ticking."

"No."

"No?"

"No, I guess not."

We remained silent and looked past each other
until my father got up to repark the car.

Horst and Elke drove to the church. My parents trailed
them. I wanted to walk and the guys didn't dare to
leave me unsupervised. The village was well kept and
clean. There wasn't much to it: an ice cream parlor, a
bank, and round faces without makeup. In the yards

poodles went about their business and posters for the right-wing NPD party hung low.

The priest called Elias a good Christian and our brother. There weren't a lot of mourners. The towns-people and distant relatives kept their composure. The employees of the funeral home had their hands folded. Friends—I wasn't sure anymore whether his or mine—cried. People stood around in small groups and looked away when our eyes met. Because I had forgotten to change, I wore a gray T-shirt and jeans. Cem's hand rested on mine. He didn't let go of me. The smell of incense and rotting flowers hung in the air.

The bells tolled and the guests fought their way through the narrow doors of the church.

I stayed put, alone. The undertakers carried the casket out of the church. I followed them and watched the casket being transferred into the hearse. The motor started. Cem took my hand and sat me in my father's car. Our car trailed the others toward the new ceme-tery. We lined up around the edges of the freshly dug grave. The August sun was blinding, searing itself into the mourners' clothes. The priest was the first to pick up a shovel. Small as a toy. Threw soil onto the casket. Others followed his lead. Spots of sunlight danced on the ground. Elke had slid down to the edge of the grave in a soundless wail. Horst put his arm on her elbow and insistently pulled her up. At the exit the priest offered his condolences. He shook Elke's hand, patted Horst on the shoulder, and nodded curtly at me. A chubby woman, the kind of person who looked like she voted for a solid conservative party to avoid any deeper engagement with politics, stopped next to me and whispered, "Are you the girlfriend? He was such a young man. And so beautiful." Then she blushed. A little piece of lightly browned chicken breast was wedged between her front teeth. But Elisha had really been a very beautiful man.

Elke's restaurant was dim, an oily gloom of dark wood tables and chairs. Again the mourners were assembled in small groups. All healthy, rosy faces, their skin shining greasily. Otherwise: dying flowers, beer breath, and moist handshakes. Horst and Elke mingled, moving in small steps, receiving condolences. Some said that one shouldn't die this young and least of all of a broken bone. Older ones begged to differ: In the war . . .

Elke showed me a brochure with pictures of gravestones. They had decided to get a simple flat marker made of solid black granite, polished surface, scratch-resistant and highly durable, timeless and classic—that's how the brochure described it. Then Elke went off to say hello to distant relatives.

I went over to Elias's grandmother. For the funeral of her only grandson she'd been given leave from her retirement home. She was a slender woman with thin, white hair tied into a tiny knot. She reached out her bony hand and pulled me close. I could smell her sweet breath and the faint lavender scent of her clothes.

We got back by midnight. My parents were the first to say good night and go to bed. Cem and Sami didn't let me out of their sight. I knew what they were afraid of.

The clocks weren't in sync. One cuckoo after the other was pushed forward on a small wooden panel to screech its eerie hymn to the night. Following their mechanical bird cry, some of them remained silent on their board for a moment and stared out into the room with dull eyes. Then the mechanism kicked into motion again. The bird disappeared into the clockwork and then another one shrieked. At ten past twelve it was over.

"Dude," said Sami.

"Germans," said Cem.

"I'm going to bed."

"Me, too."

"Masha?"

I said I'd have a cup of tea before bed. I opened the door leading out to the deck and sat outside. It was a clear night and with my finger I traced the constellations of the stars, just as I had with my father when I was little.

The next morning we drove back home. Father sped way past the speed limit. I looked at him and didn't understand how he could still be alive and Elias could not. The landscape rushed past and never changed much. Fields, grassland, rest stops whose McDonald's signs looked like the crescents on minarets. Next to the highway a carnival was in the process of being broken down, a half-assembled Ferris wheel reaching up into the cloudy sky.

4

My immune system gave out shortly after the funeral. Everything hit me—partly in succession, partly at the same time: an inflammation of the middle ear, bronchitis, a stomach flu, migraine. My body was giving up. I did nothing to get better, but a death wish alone wasn't enough. I lay in bed and stared at the ceiling. The paper planes that Elisha had made for me because I loved mobiles were still hanging there. I knew neither what day nor what time it was. I wasn't even clear about the month. I lived in a vacuum. Sometimes I forgot that Elisha wasn't there. Sometimes I waited for his key to turn in the lock. To hear his footsteps on the floor.

Cem and my mother gave me medicine and forced me to eat. Sami often sat next to me and looked like the world had just ended.

5

On Christmas Eve I strolled through the park, along the Main riverbank and its backdrop of skyscrapers, museums, and darkly painted benches. It was the perfect night for outdoor exercise. The only people out on the streets were Muslims, Jews, and a few lonely Christians. My legs were heavy and tired, and in front of me a couple strolled slowly. Their kid cried, looking distinctly like a moth in its yellow snowsuit. Trying to pass, I tripped over a tree root and fell onto my hands and knees. The acute pain brought tears to my eyes. The kid clapped excitedly and stopped crying. My pants had torn and my palms were scratched. I cursed, climbing slowly to my feet. A pair of eyes and a hijab

were focused on me. The man asked if I was OK. I nodded and he nodded, too. The woman quickly produced
a pack of moist wipes from her bag, came toward me,
and handed them to me. When I reached out to grab
the wipe, she took my hand and proceeded to clean
my wound. Her movements were fast and precise. I
thanked her. Then I went home where I wanted to tell
Elisha everything while he washed out my wound. He
would put his arms around me, caring and lovingly.

"What happened?" My mother sat on the stairs facing
my front door, legs tucked up. Gigantic shopping bags
stood at her feet. She came every night around six, an
aluminum foil–covered bowl in hand.

"Nothing. I slipped."

"Can't you pay more attention?"

"Mom."

"Seriously, you'll have to take better care of yourself. You hardly eat, never clean, and don't even bother
to put on makeup anymore."

"Mom."

"I know that I'm your mother. As if that was any
help to you."

I unlocked the door with my stiff, cold fingers and
let my mother go in first. She put down her bags, took
off her coat and shoes, and put on the slippers she had

brought for herself a while ago. Then she went on to fill my kitchen shelves and the fridge with milk, yogurt, cereal, bread, oranges, vegetables, and chocolate pudding.

"Did you know it's Christmas?"

"What do we care?"

Mother rummaged through my drawers. She thought she knew what was best for me and took advantage of the fact that I had no energy. She found the drawer with the dish towels, took one out, held it under cold water, and cleaned my cuts. Then she poured a generous helping of iodine over my hands.

"By the way, what I meant to tell you," said my mother, "I looked at your sheets. You don't wash them properly. I don't know what you're doing wrong, but as it is, they're going to tear in five years."

I looked at her, thankfully, and laughed out loud. Her face was full of tenderness.

Mother watched me eat. She herself did everything to remain underweight. We sat in the kitchen and Mother smoked one of her long white cigarettes, which in her case looked slightly frivolous. I opened a bottle of Georgian wine and mother spoke in a serious, calm tone that she must have prepared beforehand: "I'll help you sort out his things."

"No."

"Then I'll do it myself."

Again, I refused, this time perhaps louder and with more force than strictly necessary. In the apartment above us, children sang "Stille Nacht." An off-key recorder accompanied them. A moment of silence followed the song. Then a man yelled something that I couldn't make out. Then the woman. The kids cried. My mother and I sat and listened as doors banged upstairs.

"I had planned on giving your neighbors almonds. For Christmas. But I didn't get around to it."

The recorder started over with "Stille Nacht."

"I tried my best. You had everything you needed to become a happy child," my mother said.

"I know."

"Your father was one of the first who had to go. They pulled all Russians from the ministry and sent them as nonpartisan observers to Karabakh. I didn't even know if he was still alive. Well. Supposedly the Russians were neutral, but the Azerbaijanis thought your father was an ally of the Armenians and the Armenians thought he was an ally of the Azeris."

The neighbors got louder and louder.

"Afterward—" She didn't say after what, but I knew what she meant. "It was just you and me. You didn't say a word, didn't even look at me. I wasn't allowed to touch you either—a little like now. You were like a stranger, and you lost all warmth. You never got it back. From that day onward you became withdrawn and I never regained access to you. It's absurd. I didn't want to let you go. I knew it was wrong, but what should I have done? We had a dead body in our house."

"It's not your fault."

Mother raised her eyebrows.

"It's me. Everyone around me dies."

"That's nonsense."

"It's not."

"Yes, it is."

"I had an abortion."

"When?"

"When I was together with Sami. Shortly before I left him. I didn't get my period and my first thought was that I'll have to make an appointment and somehow find the time for an abortion between my exams. Then I did a test and it was positive."

"I had no idea."

"It didn't even occur to me to keep the child. I was embarrassed about that. In the clinic the hallways were decorated with pictures of kids. Pink babies everywhere. Can you imagine that?"

"Did anyone go with you?"

"Cem. Everyone thought he was the father and was afraid of the responsibility. He didn't deny it."

"Where was Sami?"

"In the States. I never told him."

6

"You look horrible," Cem said.

In those last weeks I hardly left my apartment. I watched TV and occasionally flipped through books, magazines, or the phone book. My cellphone remained off and I didn't check the mail anymore. I had not gone to work and had forgotten to request an extension of my scholarship. My mother paid for our—now my—rent. I knew things would have to change soon.

"I slipped," I answered guiltily.

"Can't you pay more attention?"

"My mother said the same thing."

"Gee, Masha. You look like an abused wife. Seriously, pay attention. Otherwise I won't go outside with you anymore."

"Are you afraid?"

"Do you want me to get deported?" Cem went into the kitchen and poked his head into the fridge. He dug through the drawers, examining the vegetables, throwing away some and checking the expiration dates on the yogurts.

"You went shopping. Very good."

"That was my mother."

"Good woman."

"And I'm not a good woman?"

"No."

"No?"

Cem paced the living room, looking around. He tried to estimate how much of Elisha's stuff was still there.

"No." He shook his head decidedly. "You know, when a Turkish guy and a girl meet for the first time, and the girl—of course, Turkish as well—offers him cake or something else, the guy takes a taste. And then he decides whether she's a good woman or not. If not he can at least cast her out before it's too late." Cem looked me directly in the eye. "Masha, not even the slightest chuckle?"

"Cem?"

"What is it?"

"Will you tell me how your brother died?"

"No." He looked determined as he sat down next to me and pulled Zigzags and a small round can from his jacket pocket.

"Afghan Black, with very best wishes from Konstantin." Cem let me smell the hash.

"Did he get it in the park?" I asked.

"From his cousin."

"I was in the park the other day with—" I interrupted myself. Cem's face hardened. I took a deep breath and continued. "I guess it's been a while. Anyway, there were only thirteen-year-olds trying to sell me rosemary. I thought the kids belonged to the same group of guys I bought from in the past and told them in Turkish that they should do their homework instead of trying to fuck with hardworking people. One of them said that he only spoke German and the other called me white trash."

Cem laughed at me.

"So Konstantin's cousin doesn't sell there anymore?"

"No, he works from home now. He just enrolled in economics."

I took several deep tokes and passed the joint to Cem.

"Masha, I spent three hours in the booth today, interpreting French parliamentary speeches. If I don't start studying at night, too, I'll never pass that exam."

Cem was my co-interpreter. We took turns, thirty minutes at a time, and together interpreted conferences in soundproof booths. We were well attuned to each other, immediately noticing if the other struggled with a word or an expression, sometimes helping or taking over early. Even our voices complimented each other nicely.

"Do you know the French term for *synced election cycles*?" Cem asked.

I reached out for the joint again and again. My limbs grew heavy. Cem always got silly on drugs: "Continuous campaigning, federal budget, referendum, *diéte fédérale allemande, mandats directs et mandats de listes.*" He giggled.

From then on I went back to spending my mornings in the interpretation booth, where I listened to absurd speeches on renewable energy, income tax, and fish farming over my headphones and repeated the words into the microphone in German, Russian, or French. Even though I was concentrating, half an hour later I had forgotten what the speaker had talked about. I spoke without forming a single thought. My brain was a machine. The afternoons I spent in the library, sitting at a long table between dozens of other students and studying vocabulary. In the evenings I read scientific papers and articles. In the morning before classes I read newspapers and magazines in English, German, French, and Russian. I tried to fill the void with vocabulary.

7

On New Year's Day Sami came by, unannounced. His hair was shortly cropped, about as short as his beard. He was wearing a parka, beat-up jeans tucked into heavy boots, and a neatly ironed bright blue shirt.

He followed me into the living room and sat down on the couch. He opened the bottle of wine that he had brought and we watched a movie on TV.

Sami had been born in Beirut during its civil war. Albert, Sami's father, was Swiss, the son of Italians who later became French. He was the manager of a bank in Beirut. Shortly after Sami's birth they were relocated to Paris and French became Sami's real mother tongue. When he was thirteen, the family moved to Frankfurt. When he spoke Arabic, he always had to rely on French words to fill in the gaps. Beirut he only knew from short trips, images in the papers, and his mother's long phone calls with Lebanese relatives that always ended in her crying.

Sami had an older brother, Paul, from his father's first marriage. Albert's second wife, Sami's mother, treated Paul and Sami the same. Her favorite child was her youngest, born after their arrival in Frankfurt, whom she had named Leyla. Neither Sami nor Paul were jealous of Leyla. They both loved her sincerely and boundlessly. When Paul graduated from high school, Albert decided that it would be better for Paul to study economics in the United States. So Paul went to California. Sami had spent every summer with his older brother and soon moved in with him in the States in order to get his high school degree there. In his new school none of his classmates could figure out why he had both a hard German accent and an Arabic name. He was supposed to return to Germany, but didn't because he fell in love.

A few weeks after arriving in the States, Sami met Neda. She was fourteen, had long, black hair, almond-shaped eyes, slender ankles, and, to Sami, she was unreachable. They became friends and sometimes went to dinner or to the movies, but Sami wasn't even allowed to hold her hand. Neda fell in love with Paul, who didn't much care for her, and besides, he would never have betrayed Sami. Sami and Neda remained friends. Sami finished high school and went off to college in a different city in California.

Two years passed and on one warm spring day when the campus was fragrant with lilac they happened to see each other again. Neda wore her hair down and—inevitably—a romance ensued. Except that Neda was from a traditional family. Her parents expected her to marry the older Persian doctor who had been chosen for her. Sami supposedly had a lot of women and supposedly he was looking for Neda in every single one of them.

When I fell in love with Sami, Neda had been married for a month and Sami had just returned to Germany to get his master's degree. I had worked up the courage to talk to him at a bar. He had sat with a friend two tables down and hadn't even looked at me. I was insanely bored that night. I was there with a woman who crushed my hand and had got her Ph.D. in gender studies. I had known about Neda from the very beginning and I also knew that Sami would return to California in two years to get his Ph.D. We stayed together for those two years and I loved Sami in a way that I had never loved anybody before, and he loved the memory of Neda.

I had asked him if he compared me to Neda. It was
a lazy Sunday morning, the bedroom draped in a wan
gray light. We were lying on the bed. He was reading the
Sunday paper, I was reading a dictionary. Now and then
I read a word out loud and he corrected my Arabic pro-
nunciation. Sami said that he didn't think much of com-
parisons, and anyway, Neda and I were too different. I
wanted to know what he meant. He explained that I was
strong and independent. That I didn't really need him.
That Neda was fragile. He had fallen in love with her the
very first day, and when he saw how she suffered it broke
his heart. Crocodile tears, I said. She left you. I didn't
have the energy to stop her, Sami said. Did he compare
our bodies, did he think of Neda when he was lying in
bed next to me? Or when he was making love to me, did
he think of her then? Sami got up and left the room. He
didn't even slam a door. He left, quiet and determined.
But if somebody tells you that he loves another woman
and if she happens to love him as well, there's no use in
going on talking, especially if you love him.

I had searched the Internet for photos of Neda and
finally found one on a social network. Neda wasn't particularly pretty and what she had written on her page
wasn't particularly smart. For a while I had her picture
up next to my mirror and compared our faces in the
morning, afternoon, and at night. I wanted to understand why he loved her and not me.

Sami had fallen asleep during the movie. When the credits rolled I placed a blanket over him and turned the TV off. He woke up.

"I'm going to go home now."

"You can stay."

With great effort he propped himself up: "No, I'm going to drive now."

"You can't drive. You've had too much to drink. Sleep here."

"Seriously?"

"Yes. I'll wake you up tomorrow."

"Thank you."

"My pleasure."

Sami turned toward the back of the sofa and went back to sleep.

8

At my oral exam for my diploma, Windmill put on a presidential demeanor. I focused completely on the buzzing of the fly in the room, its shiny green body that looked more like a tank than something air-bound. I had passed with top marks and didn't know how that had happened. They asked me where I'd like to work and I said the United Nations.

Didn't I know how hard that was?

Had I not just graduated with top marks?

Windmill laughed.

I had prepared thoroughly, learned the most important UN languages and done the right internships. I was good, I said.

Nothing wrong with my grades, he replied.

"But truly, how good is your Arabic?" Windmill asked.

"Quite good," I lied.

"And you just learned it on the side?"

"No."

"What? No?"

"Not on the side. As a double major."

"Your strongest dialect?"

"Lebanese."

A week later Windmill called to say that I'd graduated at the top of the class. Then he went on to praise my interpreting notes and invite me to dinner. I agreed, without quite knowing why.

We sat in an Italian restaurant across from the Alte Oper. Windmill looked at me as if he was afraid I was going to start crying. It was easy to read in his face that he hoped it wouldn't happen in the restaurant.

On the menu there were no prices and few dishes. The plates were served and cleared in next to no time. To be precise they were cleared before we had a chance to finish. Windmill kept saying, "You've got to try this!" And kept on ordering more, always in Italian, always winking and joking with the waiter. I tried to discern in which region he had learned Italian, but couldn't—his

Italian was clear and sterile. Without so much as a trace of an accent. Soulless, as if bred in a lab.

"Where'd you learn Italian?" I asked.

"In Mayence, at the university. And you?"

He focused on me as if we were back in the exam.

"In Rimini."

"What did you do there?"

"Waitressed for three summers."

Windmill nodded and signaled to the waiter that he could now serve the espresso. The cups were made of porcelain that was so white it was almost transparent. I leaned across the table and kissed him. He was surprised but returned my kiss.

"I don't like their espresso here. Don't you agree? I'll make you a better one at home."

He paid the check discreetly with his credit card, which I found a pity as I would have loved to know what I was worth to him.

In the dimly lit hallway I discovered that Windmill was the kind of man who first pulled a woman's hair and then kissed her. His touches were mechanical and predictable. I looked at his body, how it lay on mine. I saw him kiss my forehead, nose, and lips. Tenderly, and just a little greedily. I saw him unbutton my dress and me helping him. I saw him touch my inner thighs, push aside my panties, lay his hands on my vagina, him putting on a condom. And then I saw him lift up my pelvis, felt the penetration and winced. He interpreted this as a sign of lust and moved faster inside me. I pushed him away.

I went into the bathroom and looked at myself in the mirror for the first time in a while. I was naked and thinner than I had ever been. I had no hips. The ribs were clearly discernible and my stomach was caved in. I was disgusted by myself and the man I'd just fucked. He had used me and I had let it happen. I felt empty, sure that this was the low point of my life. But then I looked around the blue-tiled bathroom, and not only did I find a shower with a natural stone floor, but also makeup remover and a brush with long blond hair in it, and felt even worse.

On my way home I sat by myself in an empty S-Bahn car and watched raindrops burst on the windows.

9

Most days Cem came by around ten in the morning. When I heard him turn the key in the door I was already in the kitchen, waiting for him. My mother must have made a copy of my keys for him.

"You won't believe this," Cem said and threw his coat over the back of a chair. His coat gave off a little of the cold outside.

I didn't inquire, only waited as he put the coffee-maker on the stove and heated some milk.

"My dad went to a CDU meeting yesterday."

Outside, thick snowflakes fell. I watched them through the window, unwilling to believe what he'd just said.

"He went where?"

"To the CDU. The Christian Democratic Union. The conservatives." When Cem thought he saw the appropriate reaction in my face, he continued: "It was about integration. When Baba read *Der Spiegel* and *Das Bild* he got scared. Of the Islamists, mind you. My *teyze* tried to explain to him that, statistically, he'd probably be considered an Islamist as well. But he didn't listen to her. Said he wasn't even a Muslim. Then he read an article by a CDU secretary general and wanted to hear my mother's take on the whole affair. She said that he should take out the trash."

"Did he do it?"

"What?"

"Did he take out the trash?"

Cem waved this off: "He went. To the CDU campaign rally. The room was packed. Only whites. In the middle of the room he spotted another *kanack* and tried to make eye contact with him. But the other one was embarrassed and looked away. The secretary general first praised the foreigners, saying they supply the export world champion with necessary skills. Due to the overidealized multicultural reveries of the Social Democrat / green coalition, Germany has lost a lot of time. The days of window dressing are over. Those who don't meet their responsibilities as an immigrant should no longer expect tolerance. We will confront those who refuse to integrate. To that end we need a strong state—which is also in the interest of the immigrants observing the law. Baba felt like this was directed at him and nodded his head in agreement. And it went from there. Hundreds of thousands of immigrants who refuse to integrate, who—despite some of them being well educated—make the conscious decision to seal themselves off from their German environment. Xenophobia and Germanophobia winding each other up. And warnings of false generalizations or referrals to a successful integration somewhere else don't help those Germans concerned about the progress of their own children. Especially with schools that hardly have German students anymore—and it's the same for preschools. And it also doesn't help those who are afraid of violent attacks when their children are on their way to school or in the subway. Not at all. Therefore, we have to make it clear that we are seriously confronting the growing resentment toward deficiencies in the coexistence of Germans and immigrants. We have to ask ourselves whether the sanctions that we pushed through are applied consistently or whether they will have to be increased—for example, when someone drops out of an obligatory integration course. Faith plays a big role for many immigrants, especially those from predominantly Muslim countries. As do social and cultural practices informed by faith. They have the same freedom of religion as we Christians do. But at the same time there cannot be a religious or cultural blank check when it comes to basic rights: gender equality and nonviolence in families. And if—as is proven by scientific studies—younger, religiously active Muslims in particular show violent behavior, Muslim organizations in Germany must take a firm stand on this. It is not enough to caution against Islamophobia. Successful integration demands plain language instead of window dressing, consistent action instead of exclusion. Cosmopolitanism, mutual respect, and law and order belong together. The coexistence of people of different cultures and religions requires a strong sense of identity. And this includes embracing our Christian tradition as a basis. Baba came home a broken man. Hadn't known that it was that bad."

"What now?"

"I don't know. He spends all his time in front of the computer, looking for real estate in Turkey. Having been in Germany for forty-two years, he just now learned that he's a Muslim."

10

The next day I went to Windmill's office. His secretary was surprised to see me and asked whether I had made an appointment.

For a brief moment I stood in front of her, a little hesitant. The wall behind her was full of pictures of Windmill either standing or sitting next to important people. For a moment I stared at her, irritated, then went into his office and sat down in one of the visitor chairs facing his desk. As always Windmill was wearing a perfectly ironed white shirt, leaving the top three buttons open. He immediately stopped filling out whatever forms he was filling out and gave me an insecure smile.

"Why don't you turn on the radiator?"

"It's not snowing anymore."

"It's cold."

"I didn't think I'd see you again this soon," he said.

"I need a job."

"Those are a little rare at the UN these days."

Windmill's expression turned to amusement. I couldn't name a reason why he should get me a job, but it was worth a shot. His office was as cold as Lenin's tomb. The interior decoration was neutral and predictable. A soft, lightly colored carpet, a desk with a glass top, above which hung an abstract painting. A large one.

"I want something in Israel."

"Why Israel of all places?"

"Are you Claude Lanzmann?"

Windmill grinned and I quietly closed the door behind me.

11

Sami parked in the driveway at my house. On the phone I'd explained to him that it was urgent and he'd borrowed his father's car—a large black company car whose sole raison d'être was to impress.

When I put on the seat belt Sami gave me a concerned look. His eyes went from gray to green to brown, depending on the light and angle. Now they were red from exhaustion. Sami started the car. I rolled down the window and turned the radio all the way up. The full moon shone.

I easily found the path along the narrow rows. Elisha's marker was clean, with fresh flowers on top. I took a

small marble from my pocket and put it on the gravestone. Sami stood back and didn't let me out of his
sight. Eventually he did go back to the car, though.
"I'm sorry," I said to Elisha. I lay down on the marker,
reaching out for him.

I had photos with me: two that Elisha had taken
of me and two mirror shots of myself that I had taken
after his death. I dug a hole next to his gravestone, put
the photos inside, and lit them on fire. The photo paper
burned quickly and two minutes later it was all over. I
shoveled dirt over the hole and flattened the soil.

A few hours must have passed. Sami took me in
his arms and carried me to the car. I hugged him and
immediately let him go again. We sat silently in the
car for a while. Then he pulled the keys from the ignition. He turned toward me, reached out for my hands,
turned the palms face up and put them on his cheeks.
I remembered his smell and the feeling of kissing him.
When our lips almost touched I pushed him away with
full force. His head hit the side window. I got out and
ran up the road. At some point I stopped and went
back to the car. Sami sat on the hood. The hurt look on
his face startled me.

"I don't know. I'm sorry," he said.

"Did you hurt yourself?"

"I'm so sorry."

"I can't," I said.

"I know."

I took his hand and hugged him, our mouths coming close again. Nothing happened.

We went for a walk through the village, wandering the streets in which Elisha had played as a child. Past the detached houses with closed shutters, past his parents' restaurant, the post office. We crossed a schoolyard, stopping in front of a basketball hoop. No drunk teenage townies in sight. We looked out onto the dark water of the river that ran through the village, its name unknown to us. At the gas station we bought ice cream. The cashier asked Sami where he was from. Frankfurt, said Sami. No, where he was *really* from. I asked her what she meant. She smiled, a little lost. We tore the packaging off the ice cream. Mine was covered in dark chocolate and almonds, Sami's was a hazelnut cone.

"Come on, tell her," I teased. The cashier was ravenous for some exoticism.

"I'm from Madagascar," Sami said. "We all live in tree houses there and eat nothing but bananas."

"His first time trying ice cream," I said. Sami grinned at me. At least things between us were good again.

The day began, the sky grew brighter, and the glowing neon sign for the autobahn rest stop was turned off. We shared the rest stop with a group of German soldiers. Their uniforms looked like oversized camouflage pajamas and they ate burgers. Entire meal deals with fries, chicken wings, and ice cream. Bellies hung over belts, and the thought crossed my mind that the uniform says a lot about the state of an army. Despite the fact that it was a German uniform, the soldiers looked like big, lazy animals. I couldn't imagine that they had the license to kill and die somewhere, let alone by choice. I asked myself whether they in all seriousness expected me to respect them for that and I also asked myself whether they thought of African-Americans on their shooting ranges and yelled *Motherfucker.*

"I have the visa," Sami said.

"Oh," was all I could think of as a reply.

Sami regarded me curiously. "After a year. Can you imagine that? I waited for an entire year."

"You lost an entire year."

He looked at me. "It was good that I was here. Because of you." He took a little pause. "All I'm saying is that I'm no terrorist. There was no reason to sleep on my parents' couch for an entire year. I'm writing my thesis on German idealism. I taught at the university. I had friends and something like a girlfriend."

"Oh."

"She dumped me when it became clear that I wouldn't be back for a while."

"I'm sorry."

"You don't have to be."

"Have you heard anything from Neda?" I tried to say this as casually as possible, but my voice trembled.

"No. What makes you think that I would?" Sami asked, genuinely surprised.

"So, you're leaving?"

"Yes."

"When?" I swallowed, trying to keep a business-like tone, but the word shook.

"Next month. What are you going to do?"

"I got a fixed-term contract with the Tel Aviv office of a German foundation. I shouldn't worry about Hebrew, they said."

"But you know Hebrew."

"No."

"Why not? You're Jewish. And your family lives in Israel."

"Distant relatives. With the exception of one of my cousins. I never learned Hebrew."

"First time that you admit to not being able to do something." He smiled at me and then said: "Let's go, I'm tired."

12

I started packing everything into boxes. On some I wrote my name, on most the names of Elisha's parents. More than half a year had passed since his death and his parents had regularly sent me postcards reminding me to send Elisha's things. The postcards displayed Thuringian landscape shots. They came every week and in white envelopes, so that their content wouldn't force itself upon the mailman. After a while the motifs started to repeat themselves. The cards were always written with a black ballpoint pen and in Horst's narrow handwriting. Polite nothings became increasingly rare and often some words were illegible, because Horst was probably drunk and wrote them in phases of emotional turmoil, complaining about the injustice done to him. I didn't understand why, among all the options, he chose Thuringian landscapes. Thuringia had nothing to do with our subjective sense of justice.

It was not for me to judge, but Horst was anything but a good father. He drank away the proceeds from his wife's restaurant and now and then coached the local soccer team. Elisha, never one to excel at sports, got a beating after every game. The way he saw it, the coach's son shouldn't grow up to be a weakling, or a homosexual. It had taken Elisha a while to comprehend that love isn't expressed with fists.

Explaining to Horst or Elke that I needed Elisha's things had been impossible. I needed his things close by, because I would roam our apartment for hours and days on end, telling myself that Elisha would come through the door any minute.

Now I stood in this very apartment, from which I had never ever wanted to move, and packed. It had taken Elias and me a long time to find an apartment. Mostly it was us and thirty other couples looking at a place that was inevitably way too expensive. And then Elisha criticized the layout, the colors, the floor, and the light. If his expression grew sour before we even got up the staircase, I assumed it was my fault.

I started with the kitchen, a big sunny room, semi-professionally equipped. We had all kinds and sizes of plates, bowls, serving dishes, glasses, forks, knives, spoons, pans, casserole dishes, baking pans, a pasta maker and a rice cooker, but not two matching plates. Our dishes and cutlery had migrated to our kitchen piece by piece. Mostly from restaurants in which Elisha had worked as a sous-chef, or from other places. And because it was difficult for two wineglasses to disappear into a handbag at once, we equipped our table with a wide variety of plates and glasses. We stole everywhere—in cafes, inns, restaurants, snack bars, in Frankfurt and on trips. Everything in our kitchen had a history: the big serving dish with the naked lady was from a diner in New York, the crystal glasses from hotels in which we'd worked, the little baking dishes from Paris.

Of course we hadn't thought of it as stealing, but rather a strike against the system. If we were exploited in badly paid jobs and our superiors treated us like serfs, then at least a few steak knives should be a part of the deal. The system owed us that much, we thought. Which system didn't matter.

Elisha was very picky about the table being set right. He always hummed when setting the table and started with the large knives, one thumb's width from the edge of the table and at a right angle to the chair. Then the large forks, the fish cutlery—if necessary, the small knives, the small forks, and the dessert fork and spoon. At this point Elisha would stop humming and his forehead would wrinkle, as if he mistrusted his composition. If there was nothing to find fault with anymore, Elisha would repolish the glasses, set the glass for red wine down in line with the knife for the main course, next to it the glass for white wine and then the water glass, most often arranged in a cluster. This *mise en place* seemed almost archaic in combination with our stolen tableware.

I saw Elisha standing by the stove, saw him sitting at the table, saw him pouring coffee into his cereal. My body missed him, reflexively my hand reached out for his and if I forgot, I sometimes leaned onto nothing. I saw silhouettes that resembled his. Sometimes I waited in bed for him to come home. He was still out with friends and had just forgotten to let me know. Sometimes I stood at the Hauptwache S-Bahn stop and waited. The entire station was filled with waiting people and I checked my watch impatiently, thinking that he'd be late again and that I would have to wait just a little bit longer. I looked for his face in every S-Bahn car. And in the line at the supermarket. I still bought double the amount of groceries that I needed.

Now I was wrapping everything in newspaper and storing it in boxes. In two days Horst would lock the boxes up in the basement of his house in Apolda. I opened the windows as wide as I could. The little herb garden that had grown in a window box had wilted.

I got lost in pots, pans, and flowers, thinking of our old apartment in Baku. How mother sold everything, how our belongings dwindled over time and found new owners. When our sofa was picked up and lost a leg on the staircase, my mother made a chicken that she pushed into the oven with a fatty layer of mayonnaise covering the skin. It must have been during the time when groceries were available again. I got to pick what I wanted to take to Germany. When we stood in front of the shelter for asylum seekers we had three suitcases and soon learned that we couldn't use any of what we'd brought.

I resumed my packing. Cameras, lenses, tripods, photometers, chemicals. Dozens of frames that Elisha had bought at flea markets and restored himself. Art monographs, sketches, notepads, drawings. I took pictures of Elisha's things, put up Elisha's video camera and filmed myself while packing.

The bedroom. I took his pullovers from the dresser where they lay neatly stacked. I had not touched them since he'd put them there. Had only moved his worn T-shirts, which I draped over his side of the bed at night. Now I put everything into a box. I folded every piece of clothing multiple times until it fit perfectly. In the pockets of his jeans were crumpled train tickets. I didn't remember where he had gone, or why. In another pair of pants I found a gum wrapper, for long-lasting fresh breath. His mouth had sometimes tasted like this gum. In between Elisha's winter clothes I found a big box that I'd never seen before. Taped shut and covered with a fine layer of dust. I didn't know whether I had the right to open it.

Besides, I was afraid. Afraid to find his notes. Afraid of what he had written. Of his thoughts. Maybe I would discover that he didn't love me. Or not enough. Ever since seeing him for the first time I'd wanted to be loved by him. I was addicted to his love, because he was somebody who loved with his entire body and soul. What if I had constructed that love, because Elisha had an altruistic tendency? He wanted everybody around him to be happy. What if he didn't love me, but just wanted to make me happy?

I made a coffee for myself and while I waited for the water to boil I took a knife, went back to the bedroom, and cut open the tape.

The box was filled with stacks of paper, held together by rubber bands and paper clips. They were photocopies, printed articles, scientific essays, a few maps torn from books, and notes by hand. All in all, an impressive, unsorted collection of material on the Caucasus. The notebooks were filled with names, dates, numbers, and, in some cases, even coordinates. On the side there were little drawings. And occasionally my name appeared with a question mark next to it.

I sat at the kitchen table and spread the photos out in front of me. Most of them were familiar from my elementary school days. Cattle cars filled with refugees, famished children, burned-down villages, frozen toes scantily bound with rags. Tents, wounds, dead bodies. Protesters, buses riddled with gun shots, smashed cars. Red carnations on the graves. Open casket processions. Aliyev the first, second, third. Azeri-style.

I put everything back into the box, rolled a joint, and put my laptop on the table. I had underestimated Elisha's desire to understand me. We had fought a lot, often about Elisha being jealous of Sami. That was something he'd never forgiven me for. But mostly we argued about me. He thought I didn't trust him, but I was simply of the opinion that what had happened was of no importance to us. I didn't want a genocide to be the key to my personality.

I'd read about people with posttraumatic stress disorders—not that I would ever classify myself as such—that we destroy the people we love. And Elisha was a casualty of that.

On YouTube I listened to Mugam, Azerbaijani jazz, Aziza Mustafa Zadeh, and Muslim Magomayev. I sang along. Azeri, one of the languages of my childhood. All that remained were nursery rhymes and a few poems that I had learned by heart.

I took out Elisha's photos and held them up, two at a time. I cleared out Elisha's desk and closet: pictures of Frankfurt, Apolda, mountains of garbage in Eastern Germany, portraits of me. In most I look at the camera somewhat distantly. Or my face is concealed by my hair. On the outside I'm hardly different from his other models. Similar body shapes, poses, posture. It was his love and his fascination with me that made the difference. I taped the negatives to the window and looked at them until the sun went down. I would have none of them developed.

13

Cem and I sat next to each other on the sofa smoking.
The apartment was empty and quiet. There was nothing much left to say, so we smoked one cigarette after
the other. The boxes waited in the hallway. Horst was
late. A sense of calm had come over me—not due to
my natural composure, but thanks to the double dose
of sedatives I'd taken this morning.

The doorbell rang. Horst was standing in the doorway. A bulky figure, with a rough face and a mouth
that made him look brutal. His hands were clenched
into fists and in his eyes shone uncompromising hatred.
I was afraid of him. But that was nothing new.

Horst said nothing. Only stood there, his nostrils flaring. We didn't say a word either. He stared at us.

"The boxes are here," I muttered, focusing on the delicate silver teapot that had once belonged to my grandmother. I poured him a cup, but he didn't take it. So I put the cup back down.

"Can I help you?" Cem asked, ostentatiously polite as always. Horst shook his head and picked up two boxes at once. His grip was clumsy and the boxes shook precariously. He stormed out. His stomps reverberated in the hallway. I peeked through the window and saw him load the boxes into a red van. Cem rolled another cigarette.

When he got back up to the apartment his forehead was glistening with sweat.

"Are you sure you don't need help?" Cem asked.

"Everything in there?" Horst asked.

Cem shrugged.

"Doesn't seem like much," Horst said.

"Seriously? What are you afraid of? Do you think she's keeping a fucking sweater as a memento?" Cem yelled.

"I'm done with you guys," Horst yelled back.

Cem's body was tense, his throat covered with red spots. He was about to lose it. I took his hand in mine, our eyes met and I whispered: "Don't. Please don't."

Horst stood in the door and didn't move. His face

was distorted with rage. Then he started to cry. First quietly, then more audibly, until his crying broke down into loud sobs. I took a step toward him but couldn't fully bridge the distance and stopped abruptly. It was Cem who took Horst in his arms and tried to console him. I stood by, unable to move or speak.

After Horst had finally left and nothing remained of our apartment—no memories, no smells—I went into the bedroom and flung myself onto the bed. Cem lay down next to me. His hand stroked my face. After a while he said, "That's enough now. You're getting up and we're going out to eat."

"I'm not hungry," I answered.

"Right. When was the last time you ate?"

I didn't remember.

Cem pulled me up, got our jackets, and put a hat on my head. We drove through the city center. The trees were bare. The heating in Cem's car didn't work and he kept asking whether I was cold, just like he kept asking what I wanted to eat. I wanted him to pick something. I didn't want to think or feel, let alone eat. I just wanted to throw up until there was no life left in me. Wanted to puke out the last bit. I told Cem. He yelled that he wasn't going to watch me slowly die. That he was at the end of his rope and I would finally have to start living again and I said that I couldn't and he said bullshit and that Horst was an asshole and I said that I couldn't remember Elisha's face anymore and instead I only saw blood and Cem yelled that I should stop and that he can't remember his brother's face anymore either, but that was no excuse and I yelled that he was lying and then there was an impact and we were both yanked forward.

An older man in a navy blue quilted jacket laboriously climbed out of the car in front of us. Cem and I got out, too.

"I'm sorry," Cem said. "It was my fault."

"I should say so!" The man stood up straight, hands on his hips. A white mustache curled over his thin mouth and yellow teeth. His maroon scarf was made of cashmere. Why maroon? I wondered.

"Do you even know how to drive? Do you have a license?" he asked Cem.

"We're sorry!" I said.

"What gives you the right to talk to me like that?" Cem asked, pulling his scarf tighter.

"Oh, now you want the royal treatment?"

"Not royal, just normal. Respectful human interaction." His voice was calm, but I knew that his patience wouldn't last long.

The other guy's face had turned red: "Pha! Absurd! Completely absurd! You don't know how to behave on German roads, do you? You're just a guest here!"

Cem stood up straight. "I was born here."

"You wish. A *kanack*, that's what you are!"

Cem took a step toward him.

"I'm calling the police." I began to dial.

"Go ahead! Go ahead!" he urged me on. "Your friend here probably doesn't even have a residence permit. An illegal. Leeching off our system. Like all of you."

"Your fascist system, of course!" I yelled.

"Which all of you?" Cem yelled.

"Me, a fascist? I'm no fascist! This keeps getting better and better."

"But a racist."

"This has nothing to do with racism! Everyone is allowed to speak their mind. Freedom of speech and such."

14

The roses in my parents' garden were in bloom. Cem was on the phone, pacing the lawn, gesticulating with his free hand. My parents looked at me with a mixture of silent accusation and relief. My mother was going back and forth between *She's over the hump* and *Two lonely old people in a foreign country*. My father had other things on his mind.

"What kind of a job is it?" he asked.

"I was hired as an interpreter for the international branch of a German foundation."

My mother stirred her tea, lost in thought. Food smells drifted over from the house. My guess was trout stuffed with thyme. Cem's gestures became bigger and bigger.

"But don't you think you're overqualified for this job? You had such good grades." My mother sighed. "You always said that you wanted to work for the UN. What about the UN?"

"Which UN? Do you think it's easy getting into the UN?" my father said and went back into the house to get more tea for himself and my mother. When he returned he laboriously sat back down on the garden bench and said, "No." Then he shook his head to further emphasize his words. "She has to climb the ladder slowly. It doesn't go that fast. First she has to prove that she's reliable. Then maybe she'll be appointed to the UN."

"You don't get appointed to the UN, Dad."

"Of course you get appointed to the UN."

"Nope."

"Yes. We always got appointed."

"Here you apply directly."

"Then why the hell didn't you apply?"

Awkward silence and rhythmic stirring in teacups followed.

"Back in my day, there was still wiggle room," said my father, who couldn't get over the fact he no longer had connections.

"Daddy, so far I've managed fine on my own."

My father shot my mother a concerned look.

"I don't need help," I tried again.

"Do you need money?" my mother asked.

I shook my head.

"What kind of an organization is it?" my father finally asked.

"A political organization," I responded.

"A leftist one?"

"Yes."

"Good. Then at least we didn't fail completely as parents."

"You really needed to attach that nice afterthought, didn't you?" said my mother. "After chasing your own child out of our house."

"I chased no one out of the house. Besides, we can hardly claim that it's our house if the lion's share of your salary pays the rent."

My mother bit her lip nervously. She feared that the argument would escalate, but my father's face relaxed again. Silently we sat next to each other and watched Cem. He yelled into the phone: "Dude, I don't have a problem with my national identity . . . Don't give me this crap again. National identity. I'm pressing charges. I'll go to court. I don't care about this nation bullshit . . . I need a lawyer, not a lecture in cultural theory. Shit, man."

"What's he saying?" my mother asked and took a sip of her tea.

"He's having a fight with a friend, Mom."

"What's wrong with his friend?"

"Cem, don't step on my roses!" my father yelled in Turkish.

On the plane I sat next to a woman and her baby, who was sleeping peacefully in a cradle in front of our knees. In the row behind us were four more children, who also belonged to her. The woman spent the four-hour flight standing, watching over her children. She addressed them in plural: *"Les enfants, asseyez-vous! Soyez calme!"* The flight attendants had trouble allocating the kosher meals. Every single one was noted on a list, but the list was off. The kids ate kosher, but not the in-flight meals. Instead, they had the cookies their mother had brought.

I had tried calling Sami before takeoff. I hadn't said goodbye and he didn't answer. As soon as the seat belt signs turned off, the Israelis got up, walked around—looking for familiar faces.

part three

1

I waited at Ben Gurion Airport underneath a bunch of colorful balloons that congregated at the ceiling. I read the display panel, ate a sandwich, watched people look around, clueless. Soldiers, Russian grandmothers, Orthodox Jews, and extended Arab families. A mezuzah was affixed to the gate that led into the arrival hall. Many of the arriving passengers kissed it by running the fingertips of their right hand over it and then touching their mouth. Most faces displayed joy and great expectation. Again and again, people ran toward each other, hugged, let go, and examined each other's faces as if trying to make up for lost time. Next to me an ultra-Orthodox man in a black suit and a wide-brimmed hat dropped to his knees and kissed the ground. A young woman, holding a little boy in her arms, was picked up by an older man. The boy kicked and screamed as the man tried to touch him. An older woman lectured her grandson. In the arrival hall all the different languages mixed into a wave of sound: Russian, Hebrew, English, Italian, and Arabic. A deep woman's voice repeatedly warned over the loudspeaker not to leave any luggage unattended, adding: "It's prohibited to carry weapons in all the terminal halls." Fifteen minutes ago my computer had been seized and shot with a firearm, and now I would have to wait for a letter of acknowledgment that would allow me to apply for financial compensation from the state of Israel.

It all started at the passport check. I'd been asked about my name.

"Maria Kogan."

"Maria, of all names."

I shrugged and said, "My mother liked the name. Masha."

"Masha?"

"My nickname."

He made a note in one of his forms and studied my work visa.

Why was I here?

"To grieve."

Another note on his form.

"How long are you planning to stay?"

"As long as possible."

"Are you sure that this is your computer?" He scowled at the stickers with Arabic characters on my keyboard.

"Yes."

"You are interested in our neighbors, huh? Can I take your computer for a little test?" he said, grinning, and left with my computer.

The situation was serious. Now my suitcase had to be searched as well. This task was assigned to two young soldiers, neither of whom could be older than twenty. They were wearing translucent rubber gloves and told jokes to loosen up the situation. The girl dug through my stuff, respectfully trying not to look too closely. This earned her repeated reprimands from the other soldier, who was bald. He stood next to her, bow-legged, examining the contents of the suitcase and giving orders. Every piece of clothing, every scarf, every pair of panties was unfolded. All jars were opened. Even my electric toothbrush was tested for explosives. The fact that I'd hardly brought any clothes, but instead many dictionaries, aroused suspicion.

During this examination they questioned me. Whom do you know in Israel? With whom are you going to live? For whom are you going to work? What are you going to do? The bald soldier looked me directly in the eye. Why had I come to Israel, and why had I not come sooner, and why not forever? The female soldier leafed through my Arabic dictionaries with her long red fingernails; her tone, too, becoming increasingly aggressive. Why had I traveled to Arabic countries and what did I know about the Middle East conflict?

"Do you speak Arabic?"

"Yes."

"Why?"

"I studied it."

"Do you speak Hebrew?"

"No."

"Do you have a boyfriend?"

"Yes. No. I mean no."

"Is he Arab, Egyptian, or Palestinian?"

"No."

"What is he then?"

"Dead."

They looked at each other, irritated.

"When did he pass away?" the young woman asked shyly.

"Recently."

"I'm sorry." The female soldier showed the tiniest of sympathetic smiles.

"How did he die?" the male soldier asked.

"Pulmonary embolism."

"Was he Arab, Egyptian, or Palestinian?"

I was still trying to figure out if he'd really just asked this question when we heard the following announcement: "Do not be alarmed by gunshots. Security needs to blow up suspicious passenger luggage."

Multiple gunshots followed. The walkie-talkie of the bald guy beeped and he talked into it in a quick, agitated voice. The soldiers closed my suitcase. They apologized for the examination and explained that it had been necessary because of the security situation. They wished me a pleasant stay in the Holy Land. The soldier wanted to talk me into visiting Eilat. He was from there and knew every stone, he said. His colleague interrupted to tell me about little waterfalls all around Jerusalem. She was in the process of writing out the bus connection from the central bus terminal when a concerned officer hurried toward us.

He introduced himself, shook my hand, and apologized politely for having blown up my computer. Then he led me into another room, where its remains had been laid out. My computer hadn't really been blown up, though: the white case bore three bullet holes. The officer chewed his gum.

"Why did you shoot my computer?" I asked in disbelief.

"We thought it was a bomb. It's standard procedure with a suspected terrorist attack." He spoke slowly, as if to a child, having to explain the obvious.

"How am I supposed to work now?"

"The Israeli state will provide you with another computer."

"When?"

"Soon."

My cousin arrived about forty minutes later, flung her arms around my neck, and was gorgeous. Right away she informed me that she'd received my call while in bed with her new director, but she didn't want to miss out on greeting me at the airport. Hannah was my mother's niece. But we were a widely cast family with unclear degrees of relation and Mother was bad at remembering both names and faces. Therefore everyone who didn't earn their own money was a niece or nephew. The seniors were uncles and aunts, and the rest were simply cousins. To better tell them apart, my mother secretly assigned them numbers. Hannah was Niece No. 5 and her mother, Cousin No. 13, but she wasn't a hundred percent sure about that.

I mostly knew my relatives from photos that were sent regularly. The photos of family gatherings were especially sad—my aunts still had crumbling smiles on their faces, but their husbands didn't bother anymore. They just stared dejectedly at the camera. The table in front of them was set with the dinnerware they'd brought from the USSR. Hannah, on the other hand, was always the noticeably good-looking girl in front of spectacular motifs: the Dead Sea, Jerusalem, the Sea of Galilee, the desert.

I'd never properly gotten to know Hannah. The last time we saw each other was seven years ago, when her parents had visited us in Germany. It had been a short, relaxed visit. Hannah was sixteen, I was twelve, and she never took off her headphones. Her parents rented a car and drove from one Rhine castle and forgotten synagogue to the next. My mother had her mind set on proving that it was possible to live in Germany as a Jew.

Following Elisha's death, Hannah had started calling me regularly. At night, between ten and eleven, after my mother had left. We both knew to avoid getting too close, or asking any touchy questions or expecting honest answers. We didn't talk about Elisha's death or Hannah's daughter. Hannah talked about Israel, the landscape, and the beach, about hiking trails in the North that she wanted to try out with me and about clubs in Tel Aviv that she promised to show me. She talked with me about normal things that I didn't think of anymore. Soon I became familiar with her everyday life, the names and stories of her friends, even the units in which they had served.

"Why don't you make aliyah?" she asked.

"No way," I said. "I'd be stupid to give up German citizenship."

"OK, then at least come for a while. You'll like it."

Now, a few months later, in the parking lot of Ben Gurion Airport I was hit by a wall of hot and humid air. I felt like I'd arrived in the tropics. Suddenly I was excited to be here. I was looking forward to the work and happy that my life might not be entirely over after all.

Hannah never took her foot off the gas pedal. Behind us blinked the red and yellow lights of the airport.

"This isn't the way I'd imagined you," Hannah said and lit a cigarette. "You don't look like me at all. I thought you would look like me. No, I didn't think you would, I just hoped you would. I hoped you and I would look a bit alike."

"We're just cousins."

"But you don't look like it at all."

"Like what?"

"Jewish."

"You think?"

Hannah nodded and focused on the street again.

"Not at all?" I asked.

"No."

I secretly studied myself in the rearview mirror.

"Are you sure?"
"I'm sorry."
"It's OK."
"Are you offended?"
"No." I laughed, loud and hysterical.

2

Again and again we stopped to take pictures. Hannah was constantly asking someone to take a photo of the two of us, but despite that, we only needed an hour to cross the old town of Jerusalem. After strolling through the Armenian, Christian, Jewish, and Arab neighborhoods, we got in line to go through a security check. The Wailing Wall itself was divided into two sections: one for women and one for men. Of course, the part for women was much smaller. The heat was stifling, the Shabbat almost over, and the Wailing Wall nearly empty.

A tired-looking woman with sunken, wrinkled cheeks wordlessly handed Hannah and me polyester scarfs to cover our knees and shoulders. Hannah took a prayer book from the shelf at the entrance to the Wailing Wall and single-mindedly approached it. I hesitated and sat in one of the randomly dispersed white plastic chairs. To my left, Orthodox girls were praying, dapper in their best Shabbat dresses. To my right, a young woman in a long gray dress and a wig rocked back and forth in prayer. Her little son was jumping around cheerfully between the chairs, pawing his mother's butt and babbling. His yarmulke kept falling from his head, but he always put it back on immediately, without having to be told to do so. At the very back a nun stood perfectly still, as if carved from stone. She surveyed the scene from a distance, emotionless. Her features were rather masculine and her face sunburned. Only her eyes sparkled, gleaming with an inward focus.

So here, at the holiest site in Judaism, wrapped in a pink-and-blue polyester scarf, I could have consulted God, could have complained or wailed. For a long time, I contemplated what to write on my piece of paper, but I couldn't think of anything. I wanted Elisha back, that was all. So I wrote *Elisha* on the slip, folded it, approached the wall, reached out with my right hand, and recited the kaddish. Every crack was filled with paper, prayers, and wishes in different languages. Spanish, Russian, Hebrew, many of them laminated. When I stuffed my piece of paper into the wall, others fell out and landed in front of my feet. I knelt down and started collecting them. I couldn't resist a quick glance at their contents. Every slip had an addressee. Dear God, Yahweh, El, Adonai. I asked myself whether the missing address would downgrade my slip. But the idea of addressing God hadn't even crossed my mind, and if it had, I wouldn't have known how.

"Don't worry," Hannah whispered and pointed at the pieces of paper on the ground. "The rabbinate will bury them on the Mount of Olives."

Hannah and I sat in a cafe. She had ordered for both of us and was now speaking into her cellphone in rapid-fire Hebrew. Her voice resonated with a slight rasp. Hannah had moved back in with her parents, but wouldn't tell me why.

I tried calling the number on the paper I'd gotten at the airport, but the department for shot luggage didn't seem to exist. I was passed back and forth between the Department of the Interior, Tourist Information, and the Jewish Agency. No one wanted to buy me a new computer. Hannah tried to cheer me up by explaining the difficult political situation and listing a few of the recent attacks. She was afraid I was going to resent Israel for it so she drew small circles on my map, one for every attack—until her cartography of terror was complete.

"How's the coffee?" Hannah suddenly asked.

"Good."

"Seriously?"

"Yes."

"I find it horrible. I can't get used to the coffee in this country."

"I'm sure you could find imported coffee."

"It's not that easy. What would come of us if everyone were to buy only imported goods? The economy would collapse. No more country for us. The Arabs are having more children anyway and the Orthodox do nothing but make children. Soon we won't exist here anymore. Only the Orthodox. No, I have to drink this coffee. There's no other solution." Hannah laughed her full-throated laugh: "You fell for it, didn't you? You should have seen the look on your face. My husband looked at me like that, too. Disgusted, no matter how early in the day. I don't know what was harder on him. My character or my body."

"Did you get a divorce?"

"Not yet."

"What about your daughter?"

"She has blue eyes and a full head of dark, curly hair. A delightful kid. Everyone envies us our child. Our happiness. After the split we arranged that he'd come daily to see her. In the beginning we put her to bed together. Sometimes he came early and they would watch a cartoon. Sometimes he stayed longer and had a glass of wine with me. He blames me." Hannah's face was inscrutable. "He smelled like another woman. Then he disappeared and postcards of vague landscapes and abstract paintings started arriving in our mailbox. I figured out that he was hiding thirty miles north, in a kibbutz. Only oranges, no abstract art in sight. I took my daughter there. He was tan and well rested. Ate an orange, smiled at us. I pressed my daughter into his arms, said I had to use the bathroom, and drove off."

We had passed a small checkpoint, surrounded by flower beds. Ma'ale Adumim was in the middle of the desert, on a hill from which you could (and certainly also should) see all the way to Jordan.

A young soldier waved us by with her gun, yawning. And then there we were, in the middle of a neat suburb: flower beds, preschools, synagogues, a shopping center, and clean white houses with red-tiled roofs and white water tanks. Boys sat at the bus stop, legs apart, scratching their balls.

The Arab villages that Hannah and I passed on our way from Jerusalem to Ma'ale Adumim had had flat roofs and black water tanks. Sami and Cem had thrown their hands up in horror when the radio talked about Israeli settlement policy. Elisha had stayed out of it, had rolled joints or cooked. Always with fast, precise movements, to signal that it wasn't worth starting a fight, because dinner or lunch was almost ready.

Ma'ale Adumim was one of the largest settlements in the West Bank. My relatives weren't settlers who dreamt of biblical borders. When they'd arrived in Israel in 1990 as part of a big wave of immigrants, there was little housing space. To buy an apartment they had to take on a mortgage for the next twenty-five years. Since they spoke only Russian they didn't understand the concept of a settlement. By the time they figured it out, years later, it was already too late: they had lived through the Gulf War and their kids served in the army.

We parked directly in front of the house. At the door, Hannah entered the security code "1–2–3–4" and we went in. The stairway was bright and smelled of animals.

Aunt No. 13 had a childhood in the Soviet Union under her belt, and was now a woman with heavy bags under her eyes, varicose veins, and smeared makeup. She was into bird-watching. She shared the photos she took of rare species with other bird-watchers on the Internet. Her husband, my uncle, was still good-looking. He was small in stature and had a flattering smile. We were immediately sent off to the bathroom to wash our

hands and then they sat us down at the table. The latter
was set with crystal glasses and porcelain from Soviet
factories.

"Do you like Israel?" Aunt No. 13 asked.

I said that I did.

"Everyone who doesn't have to live here says that,"
my uncle countered promptly. Just like my father, he
bore a grudge against Jews.

"You don't love your family," said the aunt, fixing
him with a cold stare.

"What is that supposed to mean—I don't love my
family?"

"If you loved us, you wouldn't say things like that."

"Everyone here believes the whole world hates
them. It's the only thing people can agree on. The
world hates the Jews," my uncle said.

"And you? Hypocritically eating your soup here?
What do you think would happen if the folks at your
newspaper were to find out that you live in a settlement? You poison everything with your leftist dema-
goguery. And you don't even love your family."

My uncle grinned and said to my aunt, "But I do
love you."

"In Berlin, they now advertise the Jewish museum
on milk cartons," I said, because I couldn't think of
anything else.

"We made it onto the milk carton. We're getting somewhere," Hannah said dryly.

My aunt giggled, but then she turned toward Hannah and snarled at her, "When was the last time you saw your daughter?"

"My mother thinks you've got to take the first thing that comes along and stick with it for life. By myself, I'm worthless to her. I've got to have a husband and take care of my child. As you can see, Soviet thinking patterns are hard to erase. She misses my husband more than I do." Hannah rolled her eyes and left the room.

"Where are you going?" my aunt yelled after her.

"To the bathroom!" Hannah shouted and left me alone with her parents.

"She has too much of a temper. No man could stand that for long," my aunt mumbled.

The lunch dragged on. My aunt had prepared almost every dish she knew. She gave everyone a generous portion and didn't wait until it had been eaten to force seconds and thirds upon us. Hannah didn't come back from the restroom. My uncle encouraged my aunt: "Masha is too shy to help herself."

"No, she's worried about her weight," said Aunt No. 13, as she unloaded more chicken legs onto my plate.

I asked myself whether the impulse to drown the following generation in food had more to do with the

Caucasus mentality or the Holocaust legacy of my grandmother. My grandmother and her little brother had arrived, starved, in Baku. They were the only surviving members of their family. For the rest of her life she remained concerned that we wouldn't have enough to eat and every meal in her house was a feast. I think she'd been the one to introduce hedonism into our family. She had tried to instill in her daughters the philosophy of living every day as if it were their last. Nothing was postponed until tomorrow. No purchase, no feast, no caress. My grandmother had voted for Rabin because he resembled my grandfather and died two months after Rabin's assassination.

During a flight to the United States, I'd once sat next to a woman who ordered all the food provided by the airline and made sure that her more-than-grown-up son and the no-less-grown-up grandchild ate every last bite of it. A number was tattooed on her forearm. Her grandson had looked at me apologetically the entire flight.

On the other hand, eating was a mitzvah.

My aunt wanted to know how my mother was doing and when I started replying to her question she wanted to know how I liked their house. Then she suddenly asked, "Has your father found a job yet?"

I said he hadn't and she asked, "And what does he do all day?"

I decided to try and remain polite.

Fortunately, Hannah returned and said quietly, "Sometimes I would be happy if I could just lie down and die." Then she said, "We're heading out." The last sentence was loud and clearly a command.

3

It was already late afternoon, but the sun still burned down mercilessly. A whole block had been roped off for the party. The music pulsed loud and fast through the surrounding streets. Hannah and I joined the line to get our bags checked. It hadn't taken me long to get used to those checks. The only thing that irritated me was the age of the soldiers. Most had only just finished high school and were already wearing uniforms and holding automatic rifles.

The majority of the guests wore face paint to make them look like elves or fairies. They too were armed, mostly with water guns, but there was also the occasional Uzi. A pudgy man with dark, glistening eyes, his face painted red and yellow, aimed his water pistol at me. I yelled *Lo*, which supposedly meant *No* in Hebrew, and waved my arms. This didn't have the intended effect of scaring him off. His grin grew wider, he shot and I didn't avoid the jet of water. Hannah gave a loud laugh, yelled something in Hebrew at the guy, patted my shoulder, and disappeared into the crowd. The attacker approached me, also laughing, and talked at me in even more rapid Hebrew.

"*Ano lo metaberet ivrit.* I don't speak Hebrew," I said.

"Not at all?" he asked, disappointed. I shook my head and he continued in English: "That's a pity. I just said that I owe you a beer."

"You owe me an apology."

"You're not from here, are you?" He laughed and extended his hand: "I'm Sam."

"I don't care," I said, and left.

A man sat at the bar and smoked. He had light eyes that rested clear and concentrated on my face. I sat down next to him and ordered a glass of water. The bartender took my order with raised eyebrows. Hannah had long ago disappeared with a bearded man.

"The dog is a whore. Bamba. That's her name. Well, this dog's name," said Ori and pointed with his eyes at the gigantic Saint Bernard that lay stretched out on the floor next to him.

"Bamba. Like the kosher peanut snacks?"

"Exactly. But she would never touch snack food. She eats nothing but steak. Here she always begs for food and the chef spoils her every time. She refuses to eat at home now."

"Is she yours?"

"She belongs to my neighbor. But I get to take her out to dinner."

Ori ordered another beer and said nothing else.

"You're a regular here, aren't you?" I asked after a while.

"It's my second living room." Ori grinned. "I'm gonna go for a piss."

I petted Bamba's red-brown fur, then she disappeared between the legs of the other guests, whining for food. My attacker sat down next to me. He nodded at me and lay his weapon down on the bar.

"Where are you from?" he asked.

"You don't even want to know my name?"

"I'm Sam, but I've already introduced myself."

"Masha."

"German?"

We switched to German. Over the next fifteen minutes, Sam, short for Samuel, told me he'd been born in Berlin and made aliyah a few years ago. Then he

reproached me for living in Germany. He would be too
worried about marrying a non-Jewish girl. Sam asked
whether I was Russian and ordered a vodka for me and
a glass of cold milk for himself. I downed my vodka
and planned my escape, but the milk had left a white
mustache on Sam's upper lip. I stayed. He pontificated.
I was so dark, surely not an Ashkenazi. The Caucasus
folks, they are the mafia here, slaughtering each other.
Only Russian girls get involved with Arabs. Sam would
never let an Arab into his apartment, because there are
guns lying around, quite a number of them, actually.
His roommate is part of a special unit, not one that
would be found yawning at a random checkpoint.

"Don't look at me like that. I don't have anything
against Arabs," he said.

"I used to date one."

"At least you're not an Arab. I have Arab friends.
Well, one Arab friend. Actually, you're right. I only
have an Arab CD, but I like it. I really like it. You think
I hate Arabs?"

Sam worked online for a big company. Saturdays,
too. But there are things that he would never ever do.
Pork, for example. Sam said that Russians aren't real
Jews. When he said that I felt a hand between my
shoulder blades.

Ori asked in a whisper whether my conversation
partner was getting on my nerves. I repeated for Ori

what Sam had said about Russian Jews. Ori turned to Sam and exchanged a few sentences in Hebrew with him. Sam left the bar.

Ori scooted his stool closer. "Everyone here is a friend. A precious moment, rare enough. To have only friends in a bar. Get it? Now you'll have to become a friend as well."

His English was clear and fluent. I wasn't sure if it was his mother tongue. His speech melody was natural, but I couldn't place his accent. It was neither Australian nor North American nor British. Then he made a mistake and quickly corrected himself. He had spent a few years in London as a child but then ruined his British accent with American TV.

"What are you doing here?" Ori carefully placed his hand on my back. I pushed it away.

"Working."

"Seriously? I had no idea that our economic situation was that good."

I shrugged.

"I've got a friend in Berlin. He always wants me to visit. But I don't know why. On the other hand—Israel won't exist for much longer."

"What?"

"Of course not. If things continue the way they're going, in twenty years this is going to be a religious state. You just heard the guy. Democracy will be abolished.

The only thing that'll be taught in schools is the Torah. Women will be banned from the beach. On Shabbat no one will be allowed to go farther than three hundred feet from his house. And, last but not least, wearing a yarmulke will be compulsory." I regarded the slightly arrogant line of his mouth that didn't fit his sad eyes. He was joking, but his body told of unhappiness.

Neither of us said a word. Ori tried to look me in the eyes. I drank my beer.

"Care to dance?" I suddenly heard myself ask Elisha.

"Are you serious?"

I nodded and went out onto the dance floor. Elisha followed. Instead of air-conditioning they used an irrigation system. A fine curtain of mist hung over the dance floor in the back of the room. Our clothes were immediately soaked. I felt his breath on my face. I kissed him. His lips opened.

Ori called just a few hours later. I had started looking around for something he might have forgotten in my bedroom this afternoon. Nothing lay on the floor except my bra, which I snatched up. But it was too late for prudishness and so I tossed the bra back on the floor. I picked it up once more when Ori said he wanted to see me again. I was so dumbfounded that I agreed. After his call I wrapped myself in a thin blanket, went up to the roof deck and spent the next few hours staring out at the sea, peacefully rolling back and forth.

I lived on the top floor of an old Bauhaus building. I had gotten the apartment through my job and had signed the lease, sight unseen. It was an annex on the roof, barely insulated and with bad wiring, but it had two small rooms and a deck. My bedroom windows were open most of the time and looked out onto a two-star hotel. The windows of the hotel were open as well, showing different people doing the same things day after day: beach, shower, sex. Couples never showered together. It was always one waiting for the other to finish. Often the one waiting leaned on the rail of the balcony and looked into my bedroom. Vacation guests have no shame. They stare straight ahead, eager to satisfy their curiosity. Men who travel alone have a tendency to take pictures of women who live alone in their bedrooms. I put a bar stool in front of the deck railing to get a view of the sea. The planes were flying so low that I could've thrown tennis balls at them. But mostly I preferred to aim those at the hotel guests. I sat on my deck or my bed, smoking pot, unsure how long I would stay. Maybe forever, maybe just a few months. Decks in Tel Aviv were worth a lot, and the neon sign of the hotel at least offered a point of reference.

4

Work was cozy. My employer was a German organization that kept up with Israel's political situation and supported a few peaceful NGOs. In its Hebrewized English version, our mission was called *Arab-Hugging*. The organization—like many others—had perfectly integrated itself into the conflict. If the war was over tomorrow, we'd all be out of a job. No more bragging about living in a war zone to potential sexual partners in the bars of New York, London, Paris, or Berlin.

The team was small and no one worked particularly hard. Our day-to-day was divided as follows: read the newspaper, answer e-mails, drink coffee, e-mails, lunch, coffee, e-mails, online newspapers, kill the remaining hours. If I was actually working for a change, I translated correspondence and contracts that dealt with social injustice and *the conflict*. Then I went out to the street, sat down in my favorite cafe on Shenkin Street and ordered freshly squeezed orange juice. My coworkers always had lunch together, but I avoided them and at some point they accepted that I'd rather be on my own. The few lunches I'd joined had been quiet exchanges of well-thought-out opinions on protests and the latest political developments in between bites of chicken-fried steak and mashed potatoes.

A translator was the last thing this organization needed. In truth, a good computer program would have been more than sufficient for their needs. But of course I didn't mention that. My skills as an interpreter were needed only on the rare occasions that we had visits from German guests or requests from the head of the office, and even then I never had to prepare.

The assignments as an interpreter were nice field trips to the West Bank, past piles of trash and unsupervised children. I constantly had to ask the kids in Arabic for the way, because our driver, who had immigrated only two months ago from Siberia, was using a Russian-speaking navigation system and could read neither the Arabic nor the Hebrew street signs. Seen through the windows of an air-conditioned bulletproof jeep, the West Bank was beautiful. Even a bit like Greece, with the hilly terraced landscape, the olive trees, and the bumpy roads. After a while, though, we passed the deserted checkpoints, road signs in English, Arabic, and Hebrew. Those always came shortly before the Jewish settlements, which were as alien in the landscape as a UFO. In general, these work trips had the feel of a scientific excursion to an amusement park.

Mostly we drove to Nazareth. My colleagues—leftist white Israelis—were full of praise for Nazareth. They always said *gorgeous town* and *amazing food*, but that was just their political correctness kicking in to keep up the good mood. Nazareth was one big disappointment: a small town with lots of problems and a big street market. It also boasted a gigantic church with a much higher spiritual than artistic value.

From time to time I accompanied a German delegate to her meetings in Jerusalem, which took place either in some random committee of the Knesset or in a hotel lobby. There I whispered in her ear whatever her colleagues had just said in English about the weather. With my next breath, I whispered a potential English answer into my delegate's ear—for example, a compliment on the air-conditioning. In almost all cases, my delegate took my suggestions and repeated them in a horrible accent. But at least it seemed authentic that way. Often I was haunted by the voices and facial expressions of my delegates for the rest of the day. I was sure that Windmill had intended this job as his revenge. But for the time being, I was content.

5

The asphalt smelled of rain and was just as gray as the sky. I was waiting for the bus to Jerusalem. On Friday night everything shut down—the Shabbat was holy and no work was permitted, without exception. *The seventh day is a Sabbath of solemn rest, holy to the LORD. Whoever does any work on the Sabbath day shall be put to death,* it says somewhere in the Torah, if I recall correctly. Because everything would lurch to a halt in an hour, the Tel Aviv bus station was packed. The rain was really pouring down by now and travelers pushed into the humid concourse. Across from me was a young woman in uniform, painting her nails. On the chair next to her lay a small purse and a machine gun.

To her right was a man in royal blue shorts wearing a white yarmulke that was affixed to his ginger curls by two big hair clips. Behind me, two Thais of indeterminable age were having a loud conversation. The bus pulled up and all of us got on. The air inside the bus was hot and stale, the windows fogged from the inside. As on most Israeli buses the mood was tense. Everybody watched everybody. Women and children were mostly innocuous, as were older men. It was mostly the young guys who might strap on a bomb. Every hint of a paunch was suspicious.

On the seats in front of me a couple in uniform sat down. She was taller than he, blond, slender, and meticulously made up. He had an alert, intelligent gaze and a heavy body, which he maneuvered gracefully along the aisle. She laughed at the little stories that he whispered to her in Russian. After every comma, they kissed. I was so jealous that my heart ached. I couldn't remember ever laughing that hard at anything Elisha told me, and for that, I felt I'd done him an injustice.

They were waiting in front of the bus terminal. Ori ran toward me. He hugged me and gave me a brief kiss on the mouth. There was a lighthearted and trusting quality about him, that of somebody who had not yet been betrayed. Maybe it was his age. He was twenty-two, had just finished his military service, and was under the impression that life meant well for him.

"So glad you could make it," Ori said. "This is my sister, Tal."

Tal extended her hand and I shook it a little longer than necessary.

Ori took my bag, slung it over his shoulder, and waved over a cab. I kept looking back over to Tal. She had long dark-blond curls and green-brown eyes that reminded me of sandpaper. And in her face I saw something that was in mine, too, and it didn't bode well.

We ate in the old town. En route we saw Orthodox Jews dressed up in shiny coats and furred hats for Shabbat.

The restaurant was big and simply furnished, light marble tiles on the floor and walls, a lot of flaked-off fake gold and small plastic flower arrangements on the tables.

Our waiter was a scraggy man with a thick mustache and golden canine teeth. Reluctantly, he wiped off the table with a not-quite-clean cloth and then threw menus down in front of us. When I thanked him in Arabic and asked about the homemade lemonade, his eyes lit up. Ori and Tal were just as surprised as the waiter. He asked whether I was a 1948 Arab—a

Palestinian who had remained in Israel after the 1948 Arab-Israeli War. I said that I wasn't. His long, bony, reddish face looked at me questioningly.

I caught Ori's puzzled glance. And so did the waiter, who, obviously amused, asked me where I was from. He spoke the extremely soft and almost songlike Palestinian that I loved so much, because it reminded me of Lebanese and therefore of Sami.

"From Germany." In this situation this seemed like the easiest answer.

"My cousin is living in Germany. Beautiful country. But people don't learn Arabic there?"

"I studied it."

"That makes sense. With your classical Arabic you sound like a newscaster." He laughed.

"What choice did I have? At the university we almost exclusively studied Fusha. Only very rarely were there classes on 'Amia, the dialects," I said, defending myself.

"And which dialect did you pick?"

"Lebanese," I said, and I could feel myself blush.

The waiter smiled at me. "And your husband?" he asked me.

Ori raised his right eyebrow questioningly.

"I'm not married. I'm an interpreter."

"Hebrew–Arabic?" he asked.

I shook my head. "I translate Russian and French."

The waiter nodded. "French. Very romantic, but useless. The dessert is on the house." He patted Ori's back and headed to the next table.

"You speak Arabic?" Ori asked.

"Yes."

"Why?" asked Tal.

"What do you mean, why?"

"You speak Arabic, but no Hebrew. That's strange, isn't it?"

"What use is there in learning a small language like Hebrew? If I can have a UN language instead?"

"Your Arabic isn't bad at all," Ori said. Tal leaned back and crossed her arms.

"You speak Arabic?" I asked Ori.

"Only what I learned in the army. But they don't want to hear that."

Tal rolled her eyes. Ori saw it and I could see him trying to keep his composure.

"A friend of mine is fluent in Arabic. His Arabic is better than that of most Arabs," Ori said.

I swallowed hard.

"But only because he works for the secret service," Tal said. Her dress was shiny black-blue. Gold jewelry glittered around her neck and in her hair.

"As did I," Ori said.

"Then you should know what happens there." Tal held her breath for a moment, beside herself with rage.

Ori shot her a hostile look. Tal leaned back in her chair and continued, "But you spent your military service in front of a computer. You weren't out there. You don't know the first thing."

The waiter now looked over contemptuously.

"Fine. You are the only fighter in the family. Are you accusing me of not having been in a combat unit? Should I have lost a leg for the country? Or an arm? Would you have preferred that?" said Ori.

Tal got up and left, slamming the door.

"Can't we have a single conversation without it turning into a negotiation over Zionism and the entire history of Israel?" Ori leaned on his elbows.

"I'm going to check on her."

"Go ahead. Leave me here all by myself."

Tal was standing in front of the restaurant, smoking. I joined her. A group of Orthodox Jews hurried past, their hats covered with plastic bags to protect them from the rain.

"I don't glorify them. I think our culture is fundamentally different from Palestinian culture. Women don't have any rights in Arab society and there's a lot of other shit going down there. What I care about is my country. I love my country, but not its current state. I want to live in a free, democratic state."

"OK," I said.

We smoked in silence. The sun lowered in the sky—a rapid succession of pink, orange, lilac, purple, and then the absence of light. As we went back inside, Tal's hand grazed my bottom.

That night I stayed in Ori's apartment. I told him that sleeping with him had been an accident that would never happen again. And then I told him about Elisha and said that I couldn't recall Elisha's face in the dark. Ori listened patiently, without saying a word. After I was done, he gave me a long hug and left the light on in the hallway. Once he returned, he held me and said nothing and that felt so good that for a long time I couldn't stop crying. I cried because it felt good. I cried because then he pulled me closer. I cried because he wasn't embarrassed by my tears. And I cried because he wouldn't leave until I stopped. When the tears finally ceased, Ori fell asleep immediately. Exhausted. By me. I got up, left him a note, and went home.

6

A week later I was invited over to Tal's for dinner. I hadn't planned on going but then I was too nervous to cancel.

Besides, I had spent the morning with Hannah and Aunt No. 13 at Yad Vashem. Following the elaborate and devastating visit, Aunt No. 13 invited us for coffee and cake. In the air-conditioned cafeteria of Yad Vashem she told us about the renovations at her house that started with the purchase of a new TV (the same that my Great-aunt No. 7 had recently bought). Unfortunately, the TV didn't fit on the wall, so she'd had a window bricked up and put it there instead. Furthermore, she had seen a nice parquet on discount at the

hardware store and had bought it right away. Except
that it wasn't quite enough to cover the floor (Aunt
No. 13 was a little cheap) and now it was sold out.
She had to buy a different kind that looked like the
other one, but later it turned out that the new kind
was slightly thicker than the old one. Now she was at a
loss. The Arabs who worked for her said she'd have to
redo the whole thing, but Aunt No. 13 accused them of
being jihadists. And now, she said, she could begin telling Hannah and me about my grandmother's escape
from the Germans. I quickly told her I knew the story
already, as I feared we might never leave Yad Vashem.

"But I'm sure you don't know the details," Hannah
said, and Aunt No. 13 turned a gratified smile on her.

"I think I do know the details," I replied.

"Never forget," Aunt No. 13 said.

"Of course not," I said. "But that's not enough."

"What do you mean?" Hannah asked.

"Even fanatic settlers commemorate the Holocaust," I said.

"I'm a settler, too," said Aunt No. 13.

I bit my tongue.

Tal lived in Neve Tzedek, not far from the market where
I bought flowers for her. As I was paying I kept telling myself that it wasn't too late to go home and watch

Tatort or Skype with Cem. When talking with Cem I sometimes—actually, always—asked about Sami, as I didn't want any direct contact with him. Why this was, I didn't quite know. So instead, I tried to make Cem my proxy. But he'd refused to cooperate, instead repeating, "Why don't you call him yourself?"

Tal answered the intercom and buzzed me in. When I entered her apartment she was in the kitchen, preparing a big chunk of meat. She smiled at me and gave me a tender kiss on the cheek, not bothering to put down the dripping duck breast.

"I'm not quite done. Feel free to give yourself the tour if you'd like." She was wearing a black dress, very low cut in the back. A red-and-white-checkered apron was tied around her waist. As she lovingly marinated the duck breast, I studied the tattoos on her back.

"My brother would be jealous if he saw you here." Tal smiled at me strangely and opened a bottle of wine.

"You don't have to tell him," I suggested, watching my tone.

She filled my glass first and as the taste unfolded in my mouth, Tal described its provenance in great detail. The bottle was from her parents' winery. Then, with a determined grip, she led me into the living room. On the dining room table pieces of fabric and bags of wool were piled high around a sewing machine. On the opposite wall were photos of young women in various costumes—all of them large format, pinned to the wall. Her roommate was preparing for her finals, Tal explained, and got nervous if anybody touched her things. Would it be OK if we ate on the sofa instead?

She turned off the light, lit a few short candles, and disappeared into the kitchen. After rattling dishes for a moment, she returned with two soup plates. My palms were sweaty and I scooted forward to the edge of the sofa.

As I swallowed the first spoonful she looked at me expectantly. "This is chestnut soup. My grandmother's recipe. First you caramelize the chestnuts, then douse them in stock and add a bit of white wine. Once the soup has boiled down I add sherry, puree it, and finally add seasoning."

One of the candles had burned down and flickered out. The room was almost completely dark now. Tal leaned over me.

"I thought Israeli cuisine mostly consisted of salads and spreads," I said. Tal erupted in laughter and sat back.

The meat was tender and I thought I discerned cinnamon, star anise, juniper berries, and a hint of dates. Tal served rice with fresh herbs, touching my knee as if by accident. The scent of herbs mixed with Tal's subtle fragrance and I unabashedly studied her body. We didn't talk much as we failed to find a topic of shared interest. Tal kept on refilling our glasses.

A cockroach skittered across the floor. We saw it in the pool of light from the streetlamp outside. Tal jumped up and killed it with her shoe, its shell cracking loudly. She wrapped the insect in her napkin and disposed of it in the kitchen. Later, she scooted closer, brushing the hair out of my face. I turned away and said, "Thank you! The food was wonderful."

"Wait, I still have dessert," Tal whispered into my ear. She lay her hand on my neck.

"I'm not a fan of desserts."

"You'll like this one, I promise."

Tal stroked her fingernails over my wrist and returned to the kitchen, where she remained for quite a while. When she came back, she was carrying a bowl. Chocolate-covered strawberries. Take it down a notch, I thought, but she was already feeding me a strawberry. I chewed. She took my hand and told me to follow her up to the roof.

On the roof was a gigantic ugly aloe vera plant and a sofa that gave off a strong urine odor. We stood at the rail next to each other. It was a clear, quiet night. I named off the constellations, pointing to each and talking about them as if they were close friends. Tal listened, only moderately interested, and lit a match. I fell silent. The match went out. We could not have stood like this for long. And indeed soon Tal's hand found itself—as if by coincidence—under my shirt's collar. Her mouth close to mine. She pulled me in. She tasted of strawberries and chocolate.

"Good night," I said firmly and took her hands off my body. She regarded me curiously, nodded, and saw me out. The staircase was brightly illuminated. Tal swayed. Standing in the door she stroked my cheek and said, "Till soon."

At home I took as many sleeping pills as possible and stood with my back against the window, looking at my bed. I felt paralyzed, couldn't turn around to the window, knew that down on the street I would see the dead body of that woman. I couldn't bear the nights anymore. I was afraid Elias would die again, lying next to me. Often I woke up in the middle of the night, thinking I'd just heard him.

Tal was an activist. Communist. Feminist. And one thing she was most of all: complicated. Her activism and her ideology served as a facade to keep everyone out. Tal was one of the most interesting people I knew, except that I had no idea who she really was. She was a member of Hadash, the Arab-Israeli Communist party, and she was a member of Breaking the Silence and Anarchists Against the Wall. She spent most of her time at demonstrations or political meetings.

Tal had spent the first part of her military service with an elite unit that was stationed in the Occupied Territories. After half a year of training and four weeks on a mission during the second intifada, she went into the colonel's office and said she'd rather spend the rest of her life in prison than serve another day in this military.

She was not put behind bars, but in the military bakery. After three weeks she went back to the colonel's office. He gave her a long look and finally asked her to take a seat. He lit a cigarette and pushed the pack toward her. Tal was so nervous, she couldn't sit still. The colonel spoke slowly to her: "This is really none of my business—I'm just doing my reserve service here. In two weeks I'll be back home. I'm a chef. I work in a small restaurant in Tiberias and from my kitchen window I see the entire Sea of Galilee. I don't know what objections you could possibly have to the bakery."

"I want to go home," Tal said.

She was discharged from the military on ideological grounds. Three days later she left the country. In Thailand and Vietnam she tried out every kind of drug, danced, drank, and slept with other Israelis who also had just finished their military service. In India she accidentally made a cake with laundry detergent. In general she never wanted to return to Israel. At some point she was picked up by an Israeli welfare organization, whose only representation abroad was in India and whose sole cause was cases like Tal's. First she was forced to go cold turkey, then she was put onto an El-Al flight. Back in Israel, she joined Breaking the Silence, an organization that encouraged soldiers to speak up about the situation in the Occupied Territories. Ever since Tal stopped taking drugs she'd been haunted by what she'd seen and done.

She never announced her visits. Sometimes she rang my doorbell in the middle of the night, sometimes she visited me at my office. She had two Persian cats, big, lazy animals, overfed and with matted fur. Tal cared for them on a sporadic basis. During a good phase, she brushed one of the cats (never both), filled their bowls with delicacies, and constantly picked them up and held them in her lap. But if Tal was in one of her difficult phases, the animals would go without food for days on end. She treated me like her cats: sometimes with exuberant affection, sometimes coldly. We both knew what war meant and what it was like to see someone die. To let someone die. When I translated or when I drank my orange juice, I saw the light blue fabric slowly soaking up blood and the pool of blood on the sidewalk. I could reach out to her, touch her. I heard the voices of her murderers. More and more clearly. Most of the gun barrels that I saw were real.

7

The mood in the office was boisterous—our boss was on vacation. One colleague had even brought in cake to celebrate the occasion. I, too, did nothing except click through the entire Internet. Then I decided to call Sami in California from the office phone. I went into the kitchen and shut the door behind me. It was the only non-air-conditioned room in the building, so I opened the fridge door and stood in front of it for a while.

He answered on the first ring and didn't bother with small talk, but got right down to business: "I can't do this any longer. An Arab moved in next door."

"So what?"

"Come on, Masha. You know how it is. He's a real Arab, born and raised in Egypt."

"But isn't that what you are?"

"Precisely. When he found out, that's when the shit hit the fan. He started inviting me over all the time, coming over unannounced, constantly borrowing stuff and never giving it back. At some point he found out that Minna is Palestinian and spat at my feet."

"What?"

"He spat at my feet." Sami laughed. "And you know what? That wasn't all."

"What else?" I asked.

"He also gave a little speech. You fled and left your land, your houses, and your families behind. The only reason you're still alive is that you took up with the occupying forces." As Sami recited this speech in Arabic he imitated the Egyptian accent, pronouncing the words especially hard and talking so fast and loud that it sounded hysterical. I couldn't stop laughing, especially since Sami normally attached such importance to his Lebanese accent, which was softer and quieter than the Egyptian one. "Then he started insulting me as the representative of all Palestinians. You gotta hear this. Cowards, a disgrace to the Arab people, et cetera, et cetera, et cetera. And then the highlight: Your daughters are sleeping with Jews."

I fell silent.

"Masha, are you still there?"

"What did you say?" I asked hesitantly.

"That this is complete bullshit. That my daughters would never sleep with Jews, that I didn't even have a daughter. Besides, that I've slept with a Jew. And not only slept with. Loved." This last part Sami said very quietly, hardly audible.

Elias stood next to me, completely immersed in cutting vegetables, his movements fast and precise. His bangs had grown out, so that he looked a little like Harry Potter.

I choked, tears welling up. I could have said something, but instead I reached out for Elias and asked, "Then what?"

"Well, yesterday somebody scrawled a swastika onto my front door."

I thought of an incident in an American zoo: A boy was so enraptured with a baby penguin that he sneaked into the compound and stuffed him into his backpack. The penguin suffocated. Sami had told me this story, when I told him for the first time that I liked him, by which I meant, loved. He never forgave me for using that word. Rightly so, as I was to find out later.

The next day I called in sick, went up to the deck, and looked out at the ocean. The water shimmered. The air was warm. I went back to bed.

———

I forced myself to call my parents. The conversations were a drag, but I was still playing the role of successful daughter. Except that they didn't buy it anymore and had begun searching for cracks in the paint. But my grief was no illness and Israel no sanatorium. My father had even sent me a telescope that almost didn't make it through customs.

And all along, I didn't know why I couldn't just talk to them. A few minutes into a conversation and I'd already had enough. Had nothing to say and wasn't listening anymore. Ironic, as I made my living from listening. I wished that I could show more interest and care for them, but I neglected them and lied to them about the state I was in.

On the other hand, when I talked with my mother on the phone, sometimes I was hit by a longing for a home, even if I didn't know where that was. What I desired was a familiar place. In general, I didn't think too highly of familiar places. To me, the term *homeland* always implied pogrom. What I longed for were familiar people. Except that one of them was dead and the others I couldn't stand anymore. Because they were alive.

Tal and I were watching the sunset. The air covered us like a duvet. This time the sun set without dramatic changes of light. The waves swam toward the shore and the light slowly disappeared behind the bulwarks. Everything was in its place, the beach empty with the exception of a few couples and the rare jogger.

She lay right in front of me, head turned to the side, eyes closed. I watched her belly rise and fall. Two large birds were tattooed into her shoulder blades, black and precisely drawn. They might have been blackbirds or bluethroats. She had tied her hair in a bun, revealing the tattoo on her neck—four tiny Hebrew letters: aleph, he, beth, he. *Ahava.* Love. I began massaging her back, first along the spine, then the shoulders and arms. When I looked at Tal I felt slightly nervous and sick to my stomach, accompanied by a faint gag reflex. Maybe I simply had to fill in a blank and Tal was as good as any.

Tal let out a contented moan and slowly relaxed. I opened her bikini top. My fingers now kneaded specific muscles, then I stroked her back with my flat palm and finally I bent down and traced her back with my mouth, from tailbone to neck.

A military plane passed over us and left a white condensation trail in the sky.

"Maybe they're finally off to bomb Iran."

I couldn't tell if she was joking.

"A Douglas A4," Tal said.

The condensation trail dissolved. I took a sip from the water bottle in my bag. A cool breeze swept by. I lay down on top of her and breathed in the scent of her skin.

8

It was a while before I got my bearings. I'd taken a lot of sleeping pills the night before—to be expected, given the date—and was now having trouble orienting myself. I had been awoken by jackhammers. The noise invaded my bedroom through the open window along with the fine sea breeze.

I padded barefoot onto the deck to make sure that the world outside of my apartment still existed. It did. The sun burned in the sky, old ladies and gentlemen marched toward the beach, cars honked, and the renovation of the house at the end of the street was in full swing. My neighborhood was in a permanent state of noise. In the morning the heavy cleaning trucks arrived, followed by construction, hammering, drilling, and later the buses, cars, and Vespas. And the passersby contributed their fair share.

I went back in to shower. I'd forgotten to turn on the boiler and the water was cold. I dried myself off, went to the kitchen, dissolved an aspirin in a glass of water, and made Turkish coffee. I took Elisha's photo from my wallet, leaned it against the wall, and lit a candle in front of it. I often looked through his photos, and in my mind reexamined every second of our last night. Why hadn't I woken up earlier? How could I have prevented his death?

This photo had been taken in Morocco, during our sole, but long, trip together. Elisha was smiling into the camera. My face was buried in his hair. Looking at the photo I smelled him and clearly saw the texture of his skin in front of me. In a tea house, I had asked a man with a mouth full of gold teeth to take a picture of us. The man immediately identified himself as a tour guide and tried to talk us into a guided tour. I politely declined while Elias was busy adjusting and double-checking the settings on the camera. I dissolved another aspirin in water, quickly got dressed, and left the apartment.

The conference was organized by the French embassy in a hotel not far from my apartment. I hurried

along the beach promenade toward the hotel: the sea
and blue beach chairs to my left, to my right tower-
ing hotels, built in honeycomb design. The street was
crowded with taxis and Vespas. I arrived sweaty and
out of breath, opened my bag for the security check at
the entrance, and was let in. I picked up my badge at
reception and went straight to the booths.

I'd been booked on short notice, as a replace-
ment and after lots of back-and-forth. As a result, I
was nervous as hell. I introduced myself and the two
other interpreters—the one for Hebrew and one of
the English guys—shook my hand. As it turned out,
the head of our team was nowhere to be found and
neither was my booth colleague. More and more interpreters showed up. Nobody knew anything and it was
only a few hours until the conference was set to start.
We didn't know where the organizers were, nor did we
have the documents or even the order of the speakers.
My palms were slick with sweat.

My colleagues stood in a circle, looking very relaxed, assuring me that this conference would be a
cakewalk. Among them a few legendary interpreters. My shivering intensified. A colleague grabbed
my elbow and pointed to a man walking toward us,
whistling. Our head of booth had long slender limbs,
closely set eyes, and frameless glasses. His whole presence was somehow disarmingly amiable, even though

I knew that this was an illusion, as he was famous for his choleric fits. He introduced himself, handed out the documents, and assigned us to our booths. When I asked about my booth colleague he smiled mischievously and said, "That would be me."

"What an honor," I said and swallowed hard.

"We'll see about that," he said. "You're our youngest colleague and if I'm not mistaken, this is your first time working for us. I'll keep an eye on you. You have to know that this will be a pretty easy event. It's only about cultural exchange. Nevertheless, focus and hand over immediately when you start to struggle. I expect the utmost professionalism!"

From my booth I observed the room. Only three people were listening to the Russian channel. That calmed me down a little bit and I returned my attention to the speaker, watching him gesticulating on the video screen.

I was supposed to interpret the opening address of the French cultural attaché before the first coffee break as well as the initial part of a talk by a professor emeritus on Jewish identity in French literature after 1990.

When the attaché began speaking my heartbeat accelerated. I was convinced my three listeners would hear it as well. But the attaché spoke slowly and used

1

the first fifteen minutes to welcome the majority of the audience by name. Afterward, he read out the names of the speakers and the titles of their talks. Both were also displayed on a second video screen. When he started talking about the purpose of this conference my booth colleague tapped me and took over. I felt like I'd just been fucked over.

Half an hour later, I got to take over again. The attaché was still talking, slowly and deliberately, interspersing jokes that I translated quite freely into Russian. My listeners smiled. The speech was not very challenging and I interpreted at a suitable pace. My boss's face relaxed. When polite applause for the speaker set in, he even left me alone in the booth for a minute. The professor, on the other hand, didn't make life easy for me. Despite the fact that the subject of his talk was contemporary literature, his choice of words was antiquated. And he delivered the speech at a breakneck pace.

The air in the booth grew increasingly stuffy. Suddenly I was an entire sentence behind and my colleague kept writing technical terms on his pad and pushing them toward me. But all I needed was a short pause— as my speaker cleared his throat I spoke even faster into the microphone and caught up.

After the coffee break had been announced we both exhaled. The head of booth even smiled at me and asked in French, "Where did you study?"

"In Germany."

"Not bad at all. You'll definitely get there."

Then he went off to the dining hall and I locked myself in a bathroom stall for the entirety of the lunch break.

When I got home that night, I was dead tired. Paralyzed with exhaustion. The candle in front of Elisha's photo had burned down. The concrete mixer outside was still running.

My mother had left a message on the answering machine. They'd gone to the cemetery and had placed a stone on the grave for me. I should call her back. That day Elisha's death had become something final—a fact that left no room for hope.

9

In Germany the season had long ago turned into fall, but here the summer heat prevailed. The dried bodies of cockroaches piled up in the hallway. The days melted into one another. The weekends and holidays I spent at the beach or visiting boutiques. I almost never bought anything and only occasionally let a shop assistant talk me into trying on a dress. On Frishman Street I found a shop that carried old clothes from Berlin. Refashioned. Israeli-style. In general, everyone loved Berlin that summer. Most had already been and couldn't wait to go back.

I would visit Ori in his workshop in the south of Tel Aviv. The noise and intensity of the city concentrated there. Refugees from Sudan, nurses from the Philippines, artists, students—they all lived in Florentin. Ori was a cabinetmaker who channeled his love of wood into big, heavy pieces of furniture. We often sat on the stoop of his workshop, with watermelons and cold beer. Sometimes, the owner of the upholstery shop joined us. The entire street was filled with furniture makers. And our favorite bar, Hoodna, wasn't far either.

It was only my fabricated worries that distracted me. I feared that Tal would get into an accident, imagined her crashing head-on into a truck. Her motorcycle under the rear end and her ribcage smashed. Or she could fall in her entryway, or get attacked and robbed. A serial killer could sneak up on her and plunge a knife into her back. Tal would slowly bleed to death. Her hands twitching. A pool of blood spreading around her. Most of all, I was afraid that something would happen to her at one of the protests, that she would get hit by a stray bullet or crushed by a tank. There were so many possibilities. I toyed with the idea of anonymously reporting her to the police. On the grounds of her political activism, for example. At least she'd be safe in prison.

I called her.

"Are you OK?"

"Yes," she responded, bored.

"Why are you breathing so heavily?"

"I'm not."

"OK."

"Masha, is anything wrong?"

"No."

"OK. I'm at work. I can't talk right now."

"OK."

"I'm hanging up then."

"Don't drive so fast," I said.

"I'm not driving. I'm at work."

"But later, you will. When you go home."

"You're not my mother."

"I'm just worried."

Tal let out an exasperated sigh.

"I was in the West Bank. One trip home won't kill me."

"Statistically, more people here die in traffic accidents than in terrorist attacks."

"You're sick."

She hung up. I couldn't understand how I had become so dependent on her so quickly. Mostly I just called to make sure she was still breathing. I would call, waiting for her to answer and hanging up with her first breath. When she called back I didn't respond. Said my phone was messing up. The key lock. Not my fault. Tal gave me a new phone.

10

A hot, dry chamsin blew in and brought nothing good. The air was stuffy and I felt the taste of dust on my skin and lips. Ori had asked me to drive him to a meeting point in the Negev. We would take his car and I could bring it back to Tel Aviv and use it for the next three weeks. Or drive out to Sinai for a nice trip. He presented these options like a salesman laying out his goods, although I'd said yes right away. He sounded so exhausted and depressed that I didn't have a choice.

He was waiting for me in front of his house, wearing a khaki military uniform, a machine gun slung over his shoulder. Seeing him made me sick. My thoughts immediately turned to Farid, who hadn't come back either. Suddenly I remembered what he had looked like: a gangly boy with a gap between his front teeth. I saw him descending the stairs, wearing my father's jacket, which was way too big for him. A tote bag over his shoulder. I was sure I'd never see Ori again. Israel had me.

"I won't let you go," I said.

"Don't be ridiculous."

"No."

Ori laughed insecurely.

"I won't drive you," I said coldly.

"Fine by me. I'll just take the bus."

I felt that I had it in me to kill him and that I'd rather do it myself than wait for the news of his death to reach me.

"I don't want you to go!" I yelled at him. Two Thai girls shot us a puzzled look.

"I have to."

"You don't have to do shit!"

He shook his head and gently touched my shoulder. I whimpered, asked him not to go. He ran a hand through my hair. I yelled at him, called him Elias. Elias, Elias, Elias. He looked at me, perfectly calm. My fists hammered his shoulders and he stifled my cries by pulling me close to his chest. He held me tight. I gasped for air, but none came. My tongue swelled and my throat constricted, and no air came. And when I shivered and ran out of breath and begged him not to go, he tried to calm me down, but no air came. Ori carried me into his apartment, the machine gun bobbing against his back. Gently he put me down on the sofa, covered my shoulders with a blanket, stroked my back, along the spine down to the tailbone. Once I'd recovered a bit, we drank coffee and smoked pot. In the evening he left to join his unit.

11

It was sunny, hot, and humid. The moment I stepped onto the street, sweat was trailing down my skin. I sat, freezing, under the A/C unit, working on a translation that turned out to be more difficult than I'd expected. It was a sociological paper, studded with footnotes and bold technical terms. But since it was Friday and the office was almost empty, I took generous breaks. I couldn't concentrate, I looked out the window and forced myself to plan something for the evening, even though I wasn't in the mood for much of anything. I could go out with Tal—she might even agree to that— but then I would have to shower, shave, get dressed, and put on makeup. Afterward I'd be stuck waiting for her on my deck, since I'd be done way too early. She would cancel on me last minute and I would have to ask myself some existential questions. All in all, it could turn into a nice Shabbat that would stretch into desperation late at night, leaving me with no choice but to numb it with alcohol.

I made myself a coffee in the kitchen. Mushy sandwiches from an unknown benefactor were spread out on the table. I decided to buy *burekas*. On my way I saw a man slowly strolling down the street, pushing his bike. He had hardly changed. Our clothes touched in passing and I followed him. He went down the street, turned into an alley, then into another one, until we were back on King George Street. The sidewalk was crowded and I had to give way to people again and again. It was as if they'd united into a single collective body that was in my way. At the crossing with Bograshov Street he locked his bike in front of a small shop. I followed him inside. On the rails hung Goa hippie clothes in even brighter colors than usual. My throat was dry. I wanted to drink something, but didn't have my water bottle. A pair of pants over his arm, he stood next to the dressing room, looking at me questioningly. He, too, wore things that didn't match. But it wasn't Elisha. The shop assistant asked whether she could help me, her tone and volume bordering on hysterical. Colors and sounds mixed, as if a fuse had just popped in my head. I began shivering and sweating and ran outside, across the street, toward the sea. At some point, I collided with a corpulent woman. From her shopping bag tomatoes spilled out across the pavement. Overly red and overly meaty. A soldier with dimples and an Uzi asked me if I was OK. His voice beating my eardrum. I shivered and ran on. Everything was unbearably loud and vivid. I leaned against a wall for support, felt a hand on my shoulder, screamed, shook it off and ran a few steps. Toward the sea. When the panic subsided a little I fell into the sand. The sea was calm. I closed my eyes and tried to reconstruct Elias's face, but the image remained blurry. Were his lashes brown or black? And how much did his right ear stick out? The shivering intensified. I sweat and shivered and sweat. Taking a seat in a cafe, I ordered a glass of cold milk.

I breathed deeply, watching the people pass by. When they ceased to seem threatening, I went to the bathroom and washed off the sweat. I sat back down, called work, and told them I'd twisted my ankle. Then I ordered another glass of milk. I saw him, him, and only him. Then somebody waved at me from across the street and yelled my name. It wasn't a hallucination this time. It was Daniel, the Judeophile, who came toward me, smiling, with a sunburned nose and a gigantic backpack.

"I knew you'd end up here sooner or later," he said, throwing his backpack onto the chair next to mine. He hadn't changed much, except that his skin was lobster-red from all the sun and he'd gotten a little chubbier.

"I just got here from Lebanon. Wanted to get a better idea of the situation there. You were kind of right. It's not OK what Israel does there. It would be a nice gesture to give back the Occupied Territories—especially now."

"It would have been a nice gesture in 1967 as well. Or last Thursday. This is not about nice gestures. Have you lost your mind?"

My heart rate was back to normal again and the light had changed with the setting sun.

"But especially now! Just think about it!" he said euphorically.

I interrupted him. "What do you mean, anyway? A nice gesture? Not to annihilate the Jews would have been a nice gesture as well. And since when do you care about Palestine?"

"I taught in a refugee camp there. The kids really liked me. And you know, sometimes we talked about the conflict."

"And what did you tell them?"

"Come on. They were the ones doing the talking. How horrible it all had been. With Israel. All this in-justice and wars. I had no idea. You always brushed me off. They told me they hate the Jews. They wish they'd die. But I corrected them. Told them it's wrong to hate the Jews. You can't tar them all with the same brush. They were kids, after all. Six- and seven-year-olds. I told them it's not the Jews who are to blame. But they can go ahead and hate the Israelis."

12

I had lost all control. Even over my own body. I left Daniel sitting by himself at the table, went home, and poured a glass of vodka. As soon as the alcohol started to warm me from the inside, I took a shower and let the cold water wash the heat off my skin. Then I wrapped myself in a towel and drank another glass. Then I reached for the telephone, dialing slowly, as if for the first time, and when I heard Cem on the other end, I cried and hung up. He called back.

"I dialed the wrong number."

"That's a lie," Cem answered calmly. "How are you?"

I took the phone with me out onto the deck. It was dark already. Mosquitos swarmed in the cones of light around the streetlamps. A cockroach sat on the rail. I removed my shoe, took aim, squished the cockroach, and brushed its body off the rail with my shoe. I started to cry again. The tears came from my core, from my stomach and intestines, and I couldn't stop and I cried and cried. A choppy, staccato wail that took my breath away. My hands started shivering again. I was anxious. But this time I heard Cem's breath on the other end of the line, at the other end of the world, and after a while my breathing calmed again. It was only now that Cem spoke: "Masha, I'll be there soon."

Cem really came. The sweetheart. My consoler. I'd asked him on the phone what he wanted to see and he said it would be enough to take a trip to Jerusalem. And besides, he was coming to check on me, not to climb the Mount of Olives and await Judgment Day.

In the end, we didn't go anywhere. Just lay next to each other on the beach, making sure that the other one didn't get sunburned. We swam, but the water wasn't cooling and we enjoyed the shower at the beach more than we did the sea itself. In front of us a white, Russian-speaking grandmother played with her dark-skinned grandson.

"Things are not going to be easy for him," said Cem, pointing at the boy.

"Why not?"

Cem looked at me, tauntingly. "Soon he'll realize that he's different from them. He still thinks they're all the same. But not too long from now he'll notice that he's black."

"When did you start feeling different?"

"In elementary school. Fourth grade. Shortly before they decided who would be going on the college track and who wouldn't. A new boy came into our class. Pierre-Marie. The teachers were beside themselves. The boy hardly knew any German but everyone thought of him as extremely intellectual, because he was French and because they thought his German would be perfect in a week. And then I looked around at my class. Full of *kanacks*. Marcel spoke Italian, Georgi Greek, Taifun Turkish, Ali Persian and Armenian, just like his twin sister. And all of us spoke German, too. Without an accent. And yet none of us was considered intelligent enough to go on the college track. We were destined for remedial school, or—at best—trade school. Our parents weren't supportive enough, they said. I thought of my grandfather, who had always told me and my brother, Turkish is the language of the ancestors, Arabic the language of prayer, and Persian the language of love. Such bullshit. I think that's when I decided to learn the languages the Germans admired so much, and speak them better than they ever would.

To have the last laugh. About them and their cultural hegemony."

The grandma lovingly helped her grandson put his flippers on. The sea was blue and even.

"Later came the constant questions. Where are you from? Do you feel more German or Turkish? When I was sixteen I had to go to the immigration office for my residence permit. I mean, what the hell? I was born there. I even had to stay home from our high school graduation trip. They went to London. I didn't get a visa. You know what my teacher said to me? If we were decent people, we would have gotten German passports long ago."

Cem looked straight out onto the sea. Then he grinned and said, "But this little guy here won't screw up. He'll read and understand everything. All the classics of postcolonial studies, critical witness studies, racism theories, Fanon, Said, Terkessidis. By the way, I'm getting my Ph.D. now."

In the evening we went to a restaurant, both drained from the sun, and had steamed vegetables with rice. There was no air-conditioning and therefore only a few tables were occupied. But the food was good and all the windows were open. My bare thighs stuck to the leather seat. Cem sat facing me and talked about his

Ph.D. thesis. He felt guilty toward his parents for pushing back his entry to the workforce even longer, and
I tried to reassure him. An ambulance passed us, its
siren blaring. We fell silent and followed it with our
eyes, each wondering if there had been an attack or an
accident.

"How is Sami?" I asked after a while.

Cem studied my face. "He's back in the States."

"I see."

"When was the last time you talked to him?"

"About two months ago."

"Anything else?" Cem asked.

"What do you mean?"

Cem refilled my wineglass and leaned back.
"Masha, I've been watching you guys make each other
unhappy for years now. Either let it go or get together."

"Is he with Neda again?" I bit my lower lip and
Cem drummed his fingers against the edge of the table
almost soundlessly.

"I don't understand what you're doing here," said
Cem. "The beach and the food are OK. But what do
you want here?"

"I don't know."

Cem kept his temper in check, fell silent. I could
see him weighing how direct he could be with me.
Then he asked: "Did you find religion? Did you discover Judaism as your cultural identity?"

"I had to get away."

"Don't you want to come back?"

I traced the rim of my plate with my finger.

"Not yet."

"When?"

I felt so stupid, I nearly cried. I was alone in a city I didn't know, missing my friends. I wanted them to misunderstand me and didn't even know why.

"Come home."

"Germany? Home?"

"I'm not talking about Germany. You know how things are there. I mean Frankfurt, Gallus."

"That's where Elias died."

"Not in the Gallus neighborhood."

We happened to run into Ori on Rothschild Boulevard. He was walking our way in shorts and an undershirt. In his right hand he held a bottle of beer, in his left his overpriced cellphone. Cem and Ori liked each other right away and we sat down in an ice cream parlor. It turned out that the two of them had the same taste in literature, music, and fashion. We went on to a bar in Florentin, where a friend of Ori's was DJ-ing.

The bar was filled to capacity, the air thumping with fast-paced music. Most people stood around, drinking and smoking. A few were already dancing.

Cem went straight to the dance floor. Ori followed him. Cem seemed to be genuinely enjoying himself—unlike so many occasions when I'd seen him on the sidelines of the party, sourly waiting to leave. I played with the straw in my drink, watching them. They were good dancers. The beat seemed to migrate from the dance floor to their bodies.

The music got louder, the room smaller. Panic welled up inside me. I could feel it spreading in my chest, drying out my lungs and crawling up into my head.

"I have to go home," I whispered into Cem's ear and ran out.

Outside I took a deep breath, but it didn't help. I was hyperventilating. I got into a cab, clinging to the door, and somehow made it into my apartment. Ten minutes later Cem was there, stroking my palms, my arms, and my face as if he wanted to apologize for something that wasn't his fault. He dialed the emergency number.

The doctor pulled on rubber gloves and gave me an injection. I saw the needle disappear into my flesh and then became calm, almost instantly. My breathing slowed. The fear, Elisha, and the woman in the light blue dress were gone. My head felt as if it were wrapped in cotton. A gigantic Q-tip. The doctor ordered me to go to the psychological emergency service tomorrow and have them prescribe benzodiazepine. Other than that, no big deal.

As soon as I had the pills I was better. I now knew that the problem was a concrete one and that it had a concrete chemical solution. I fell asleep.

After half a day in the psych ward—with Cem repeatedly imploring me to return to Germany—we were sitting in a cafe on Dizengoff Street. I was soaking a croissant in my iced coffee, trying to recall whether this was the cafe that forbade its employees to speak Arabic. Or was it the one next door? I was tempted to inquire about it in Arabic, but Cem was not a fan of the idea. He looked at me like I was crazy, then, like a fury, brought up my mother, my father, and his mother—though she'd stopped caring years ago—as a way of threatening me. He wouldn't stop talking about Germany. But I wanted to stay and lose myself in little pieces, never to be reassembled.

I suggested we drive to Jerusalem and thought he might cool off along the way.

At the bus stop we bought ice cream. Then we entered the main hall, looking for the shuttles to Jerusalem. On the lawn in front of the building sat refugees, waiting for work. The Russian-language press called them *Gastarbeiter*, guest workers. I had no idea how anyone could find this term appropriate. Inside and around the station were many small shops that sold sweets and cheap, colorful clothes. Surly men with open shirts and gold chains nestled in their thick chest hair walked next to young soldiers in uniforms and sandals.

"Just explain to me once more, why exactly you want to stay here?" Cem hissed.

Five Asian women were in the shuttle already. One of them held a plastic bag filled with plums in her lap. The others helped themselves, chatting and laughing. The overly sweet scent of fruit filled the van. We drove past dried-out sunflower fields. The radio blasted pop music. Cem didn't look out the window, but into a folder for an upcoming conference. From the corner of my eye I read *financial transaction tax, restructuring law, structured liquidation of banks, limitation period of D&O liability for shares, protester problem.* He was probably offended.

Cem wasn't particularly impressed by Jerusalem. The only thing he seemed to appreciate were the plaques with golden Latin letters informing anyone who cared to read them about who had donated a building, a bench, or a flower bed. On our walk through the inner city, Cem studied each of the plaques, asking if I knew the donor and if I thought he or she got a thrill out of seeing their name on the plaque.

It was a cool evening and we squeezed through the Christian pilgrims, extended Arabic families, and a group of American Birthright tourists, their members admiring the armed soldier who was there to guard them. Orthodox Jews hurried through the street—men in dark coats and wide-brimmed hats, women in wigs or head scarves. Quite a few were poorly dressed and almost all were surrounded by a gaggle of children. Cem shook his head and I felt myself once again tempted to defend a way of life that I personally rejected. But Cem didn't say anything and neither did I.

The same driver who had taken us brought us back to Tel Aviv. Except this time we rode with a group of Orthodox Bukharan Jews who were carrying on a loud conversation in Russian. One after the other took the tefillin and the prayer books from their bags. The smallest one urged Cem in Hebrew to put on tefillin as well. Cem only shrugged and returned his attention to his vocabulary. The men started praying in their sing-song voices.

Three days later Cem flew back to Frankfurt, alone.

13

In the morning I found a letter from Elke in my mail-box. Her pedantic handwriting filled the floral white paper.

I tore the letter into small pieces and let them snow down into the trashcan. I considered setting the trash-can on fire, but it was light out and many people were on their way to work. And so I went off to work as well.

Kids' pajamas and panties hung on clotheslines. White-and-blue flags fluttered. Commuters waited at the bus stops, cars honked, and I thought the asphalt was going to melt under my sandals. In front of the post office—where typically there would be a crowd of people pushing, elbowing, and yelling—there was only a small group of friendly-looking people and multiple police cars. I asked one of them what was going on. Nothing much, he said. Potentially a bomb. The squad was defusing a plastic bag and they'd probably be letting us back in soon.

When I arrived at the office I felt drained and sticky. On my desk were three folders to be translated. A Post-it was stuck to the one on top. Urgent. Reports from a few Israeli-Arab groups, each of which received major financial support from the foundation that employed me. They'd finally sent over the reports on their cultural activities. A Jewish-Arab celebration for senior citizens, attended by fifteen people. A writing group for Bedouin women—number of participants: five. The project coordinator delivered a rhapsodic report of the women's meeting with an Israeli writer who wrote novellas about cats. Then the words dissolved into lines and dots and my shortage of breath was back, a hand tightening over my throat. I thought it belonged to Elias. I ran out and locked myself in a bathroom stall, swallowed a few benzodiazepines and calmed down again. I called Ori but he didn't answer. I left a voicemail and asked him to pick me up from work. He called back an hour later and asked if it was urgent. I told him about Elke's letter.

———

At six on the dot Ori was waiting for me in front of my office. He seemed tense. By way of greeting he kissed my cheek. Nothing had happened between us after that first night, but something had grown anyway. Maybe even friendship.

"Are you hungry?" I asked him.

"No," he said gruffly.

"Would you mind keeping me company?"

"OK. I know something close by. Let's go."

We got on his Vespa and he drove us to a cafe on Allenby Street.

The cafe was part of a popular chain and in front of the counter was a long chaotic line of customers, all waiting to leave with their to-go cup of coffee.

Ori had spotted a free table in the far corner of the room and purposefully walked toward it. I would have preferred to go somewhere else but something in Ori's face—a hardness I had never seen there before—made me sit down. The two men at the table next to us were having a loud conversation about Hapoel's chances of moving up to the next soccer division. But I only understood bits and pieces and didn't care at all about soccer anyway.

The waiter gave me a weird look when I asked for the Arabic menu. He considered my request a joke and continued speaking Hebrew with me. When I answered in broken Hebrew his expression turned condescending. There was no Arabic menu.

"I'll translate for you," Ori said.

"Nice, for a change!" I said.

Ori looked at me, irritated.

"Are you sure you don't want to go somewhere else?" I asked.

Ori closed the menu and threw it down on the table. "You're becoming more and more like Tal."

"There are at least two hundred restaurants on this street."

"And I guarantee you, none of them will have an Arabic menu. Can't you pull yourself together, just for one night?"

"What's up?" I asked.

Ori leaned on the table and fixed me with his gaze. "I was out with the guys from my unit today. We were invited for dinner."

"Did the food disagree with you?" I asked.

"We were at one guy's mother's house. We'd served together. Before he got killed in Lebanon. I'd planned to have a drink with them, but then you called in that tone of yours. Like you're about to burst into tears."

My voice shook. "I'm sorry. If you want to go, you should."

Ori took a bill from his pocket, put it under the ashtray, and stood up. I didn't know what to do and remained seated.

"Come on," said Ori. "Let's go."

We got onto Ori's Vespa again and drove a few streets farther. A tall, gangly man opened the door, greeting Ori with a handshake. Then he led us to the balcony. Five guys were sitting on worn-out couches, all barefoot and in shorts. Three of them had guitars on their laps but only one was playing. Ori introduced me to each of them and I was promptly offered a beer and a joint. I took both, said thanks, and sat down next to Ori on a free couch.

We sat in silence. From time to time someone brought beer or rolled another joint.

After a few hours we said goodbye.

"You're driving," Ori said and threw the keys my way.

"Seriously?"

"I'm drunk," Ori said. He had a point. I'd watched him down one beer after another on the balcony.

We put our helmets on. Ori sat behind me, his hands on my waist. I started the engine, revved it briefly, then drove out onto the beach promenade. On our right lay the sea, dark and calm. On our left shone the lights of the city. Only a few cars were on the road.

I accelerated, leaned forward, and we drove faster. Ori's grip tightened. But I couldn't resist speeding up even more, and only in the last second veered out of the way of cars that came toward us. Or just waited for them to do so.

When I slowed down and came to a halt at the edge of the road, Ori jumped off, yanked off his helmet, and yelled at me, "Were you trying to kill us?"

Maybe, I thought to myself.

Ori sat down on the curb and put his face in his palms. His shoulders were shivering. I sat down beside him, took his hand in mine and pressed it. But he didn't react.

14

Tal sat on the edge of my bed, nervously playing with the corner of my bedspread. I had no idea how she'd gotten into my apartment.

"What's up?" I asked her.

"Aren't you happy to see me?"

"I just woke up!"

"Should I leave?" She got up and pulled the curtains open. Hard, bright light flooded the room. She turned back toward me, her lips pursed. Her eyes shone combatively. She was waiting for me to make the first move, but I didn't want to do her the favor.

She stubbornly refused to love me. I didn't mind that—just didn't understand why. Tal said that she didn't believe in relationships, least of all romantic ones between two people. When she wanted to tell me something unpleasant she always started her sentences with *Motek* or *Mummy*, which means sweetheart in Hebrew. And so almost every day I heard, "Sweetheart, I don't love you." Or "Mummy, I don't want to see you today." On the other hand, she was still here. Here, with me.

I sat up in my bed and watched as she paced the room, nervously pulling out one hair after the other.

"Do you want to spend the day with me?" she asked and coldly looked around the room.

"Why? So I can swallow tear gas?"

"Would you rather while away the day at the beach?"

"I wouldn't mind that."

The last time I joined Tal for a protest, we'd stood at a bustling intersection and yelled rallying cries. We were about thirty people, almost exclusively white and Jewish. Standing around us were at least as many people who berated us and called us traitors and sons of bitches. One spit at us and another wanted to throw his heavy shopping bag at Tal. A couple of police officers held them back. I'd been at the edge of the demonstration, next to two guys who were quietly discussing in Arabic which leftie they wanted to fuck next. The lefties were the only ones who spread their legs for an Arab, said the younger of the two. A shame that they always wanted to talk politics afterward, said his buddy.

"Masha, what kind of life do you want to lead?"

"A quiet one."

"Seriously?"

"Yes."

Tal remained standing and crossed her arms. Her eyes rested on my mouth, calculating. I wouldn't give in. I was going to play all my cards. But she wouldn't be convinced as easily—nor as quickly—as Elisha.

"You just want to sit out your time here and enjoy the sun, the good food, and a bit of sex? Nothing else matters to you, does it?" Tal sat down and pulled her knees toward her.

"Exactly. My place in the sun."

"I don't believe it." She got up and started pacing again. Her movements were erratic.

"What I want is running water, electricity, and a place where no one is killed," I said.

"You were in a good place in Germany then. No reason to come here."

I hadn't told her about Elias or his death. I crossed the room barefoot. The floor was full of the sand that Tal must have brought in from the beach. She was always barefoot, in the stairway and the garden, too, and all the dirt stuck to her heels and ended up on my floors and, finally, in my bed.

"My grandmother still has memories of a peaceful Germany," Tal added.

"You think mine doesn't?"

"The demonstration is in Sheikh Jarrah. We should get going."

15

I had spent the weekend with Ori and Tal at the house of their parents, who had gone to Europe. We wanted to take advantage of the time to talk things through. Ori and Tal's parents are something like the Israeli *Mayflower* generation. Their father had grown up in a kibbutz in the north of the country, their mother in a spacious apartment in Tel Aviv. If something in the state went wrong, they took it personally. Their grandparents had illegally immigrated from Eastern Europe, prior to the state formation. Israeli pioneers who had personally drained swamps.

Their father had served in a unit of parachutists and was not what you would call squeamish. Up until the day his sister and her husband were killed in an attack during the second intifada. They had been on their way to Ori's bar mitzvah. This tragic event changed the entire family. Tal became angry and Ori skittish. Their parents didn't entertain any feelings of revenge, but instead bought a small winery in the north of Israel and withdrew—hoping to take their kids as far from the intifada as possible. They only produced a few thousand bottles per season. The family business was real estate that they rented out to tourists.

The winery was the perfect idyll, but Tal and Ori discussed politics nonstop. Because they fought in Hebrew I wasn't clear on the details. I knew that Ori had had it with realpolitik. Anyway, he was convinced that it was too late to divide the state. Tal was Tal. And their parents, who had once gone to demonstrations in favor of the two-state solution, blamed the Israeli right and the settlers, and had stopped believing in anything. The whole family knew that more people would die.

The conflict had reached its climax when Tal noticed that Ori used a shaving cream produced by an Israeli company in the Occupied Territories. She had found the cream in the bathroom and brought it out to the yard where Ori and I were playing badminton. Tal held up the cream in about the same way she would have held up a dead rat.

"Whose is this?" Tal asked.

Ori calmly dropped his racket on the grass and asked, "What's your problem?"

Thereupon Tal delivered a long and passionate speech that we would have also found on the Web site of Who Profits, had we been looking for it. Tal talked herself more and more into a frenzy until Ori took her in his arms and shook her firmly.

"That's enough," he repeated over and over. "That's enough. That's enough. That's enough." Tal burst into tears and beat her fists against his chest. She beat and he held and she beat and he held, and I was standing in the corner, clutching my racket. At some point Tal softly placed her forehead on Ori's chest and sobbed.

Later, I watched her from the doorway, sitting on the sofa, staring at the TV. Ori was upstairs, in his room. Finally, I sat down next to Tal. She didn't say a word. Her hands had chronically bad circulation and were therefore always cold, but today they seemed even colder than usual. I made her tea, which she didn't drink. I folded her hands around the mug to warm them and brushed a strand of hair from her face. But I knew all was lost.

In the evening she took a bath while I sat on the rim of the tub. Despite the warm water her body wouldn't stop shivering. I kept watch to make sure her head stayed upright. When she got out of the water I carefully dried her off. Goose bumps covered her body and her legs were still quaking slightly. She collapsed into my arms, her body suddenly very heavy, and I brought her to bed. I dressed her in her mother's pajamas and lay down beside her. In the middle of the night I heard her get up, but I pretended to be asleep and let her go.

The next morning Ori announced that he would fly to India that same day. Actually, in three hours. Tal was gone. She had left a note on the kitchen table: "I'm in Sinai. Have to think things over."

The sun was blinding. I had forgotten my sunglasses and squinted at the crowded street as we slowly crept forward. In the other cars commuters yawned.

Ori was beside me, quiet and focused, changing the radio station every two minutes. His body was tense. A Jeep with soldiers approached us. Ori waved at them. They waved back.

We were late. I parked the car and Ori stormed out. I trudged behind. In front of him in line was a group of Bulgarian tourists. Most of them wore hats with their travel organization's logos, name tags, and big golden crosses. Ori disliked all Slavic languages. The line didn't move. The tourists spoke a lot, and quickly. They bustled like confused ants, exchanging their impressions. A little girl wailed to be held by her father.

Ori cast a grudging glance. His gaze darkened as it wandered from one face to the next. Boarding was to begin in fifteen minutes. He stroked my cheek and said, "I'll try to get past them." He dug around in his bag, took out his passport, and kissed me on the cheek. His right hand lifted my chin. He looked at me as if he wanted to memorize my features.

"See you soon." I turned away from him, unable to bear it any longer.

"When I get back, you'll be gone."

"How would you know that?"

"You're a woman who falls in love quickly."

"If you only knew . . ." I laughed.

His left hand made a gesture that could have meant anything. He ran toward the counter, sweeping past the tour group. He juked the tour guide like a running back, clutching his blue Israeli passport to his chest before being tackled by two armed security guards. As they threw him to the ground and handcuffed him, I had the feeling I was in a sports arena. The tour group pulled out their cameras, but other security forces loudly commanded them to abstain from documenting the scene.

I laughed. I couldn't believe something like this was happening again at the very same airport. My laughter was so contagious that even the tour group joined in. I approached the security guards. Confused, they let go of Ori. One pointed his gun at me and I swallowed down my laughter. But then I started up again. I finally stopped for good when I saw Ori's hurt and humiliated look.

Afterward, we sat in the manager's office. Neither the office nor the manager had changed since the execution of my laptop.

On the table in front of us sat salty cookies and a thermos full of coffee. Ori kept on shaking his head and the manager kept on smiling at me in a professionally encouraging way. He wore a shiny gray suit and big sunglasses, pushed up on his bald shaved head.

"How are you liking Israel?" the manager asked, offering the plate of cookies. I took three and ate them quickly—it was the first thing I'd eaten since last night.

"You got a tan," the manager remarked, clearly pleased. He had recognized me, too.

"You think?" I looked at my upper arms. Indeed they'd turned a few shades darker over the last months.

"Suits you." The manager grinned.

"Thanks."

"How long is this going to take?" Ori interjected.

"Could take a while," I answered and the manager nodded in agreement.

"And what about your computer? Did you get compensated?" he said.

"Last month."

"Glad to hear it." The manager's smile widened.

"I had to wait four months and then I only got eighty percent of the purchase price. Not exactly wonderful."

"Do you have any idea how long my grandfather had to wait until he got his reparations from Germany?" The manager said with only a monotone laugh.

"Doesn't work," Ori said. "She's Jewish."

"Oh, then you're not a shiksa?" the manager asked.

"Her grandparents are Holocaust survivors," Ori said.

"*Ori!*" I yelled at him.

"What? If we have to play Jew-Monopoly, then let's at least play fair."

"Would you like another cookie?" the manager asked.

I took one. It was already soggy.

16

When I wasn't at work and it wasn't too hot I went on walks through Tel Aviv. That summer Jesus sat at the entrance to the market, right next to the intersection of three busy streets. The messiah was a burly guy with coarse features and long blond hair, clad in a toga made from red velvet. In the first days after his arrival he was sweating horribly and always had a bottle of water nearby. After a while a few hippies gathered around him. The tourists followed and Jesus started lecturing on the meaning of life. Now he needed a lot less water.

Tal was still gone. She didn't call me and didn't answer a single one of my thirty-three texts. Since Elisha's death, her hand on my hip as we fell asleep, our breathing in sync, had been the first thing that had felt right. Every evening I hoped that she would come back. Every morning I walked past her house to see if she had returned.

The Carmel Market provided a reprieve from the hot sun and the air smelled of fruit. Oranges, watermelons, and cactus fruit glowed. Vendors proclaimed their love for each potential customer. I flirted in Arabic and Hebrew and still paid more than old, glum Russian men who slowly slid the coins through their hands and went for a swim in the ocean at seven a.m. I also loved the juice stands on every corner, which were predominantly manned by guys with remarkably hairy arms. At these stands the oranges were cut in half and squished by the juice presses. A bit like a guillotine. The shiny orange peel fell into the trash.

Honestly, every day was equally shitty. I stared at my cellphone as if I could conjure up a call. I checked my e-mails every fifteen minutes and ran to the window every time I heard a motorcycle pass by. Which happened quite frequently, since I lived on a major road.

I made one more attempt to visit Aunt No. 13. At the checkpoint I got off the bus, but just couldn't bring myself to enter the settlement. Not necessarily because of Tal, but because of three young Palestinians who were waiting in front of the fence for an Israeli employer who would take them to a construction site.

Illegal labor in an illegal settlement. I took a taxi back to Tel Aviv.

Hannah had also lost interest in me. She never called anymore and if I called she was always short with me. The reasons she gave were work, her boyfriend, and the dog she didn't have. I didn't know what had happened, or if anything had happened at all. I was looking for a reason for her loss of interest.

Months later I ran into Hannah on the street, her belly round like a globe. I hadn't known about her pregnancy and was hurt. A week later she called and I got an invitation to the baby shower, which I politely declined.

I hit rock bottom one day while lying on the beach. In front of me sat two tourists, tightly entwined in an embrace. She was tall, blond, about fifty, and with freckles all over her back. He had only a little hair left, a heavy gold necklace, around seventy. Both were raptly watching a game of matkot, their heads turning from side to side, in sync, following the ball. When the ball was out, both shook their heads in disappointment.

The woman lying in front of me turned onto her back and I thought of Anne Frank. At age eleven I had read her diary and understood that I wasn't the only woman who desired women and that these feelings didn't exclude the others. The homoerotic passages in her diary had reassured and aroused me, just like the woman who lay in front of me and, spreading her legs, so enticingly presented her pelvis. I'd been watching her for half an hour already. The sky was completely clear again, not a single cloud, and despite it being only morning, the sun already burned down.

My cellphone vibrated, Sami's name on the display. It had been a long time since we'd talked and I was excited and excited and excited to see his call. Then I held my breath and hoped that he wouldn't notice.

He asked whether we could meet in Vienna.

"Come on, seriously? Why don't you come here instead?" I answered.

"With my kind of passport? Thanks, but no thanks. In case it slipped your mind, I was born in Beirut."

"But I would love to see you," I couldn't help saying.

"I just sent you the booking confirmation."

"What booking confirmation?"

"For the hotel and flight."

The woman in front of me turned around and was now lying on her stomach.

"Cem and I have signed you up for an exam."

"What kind of exam?"

"The United Nations Competitive Examination for Russian Language Interpreters, in Vienna."

"You're joking."

"Nope."

"Sami, I'm not prepared at all."

"Come on. Cem also thinks you need to get out of the Middle East."

"Cem is from the Middle East himself. And you guys can't just enroll me for an exam."

"Not true." Sami was laughing now. "We forged your signature."

"When?"

"Two weeks ago, when Cem was visiting you."

"Are you guys completely out of your minds?"

"Are you coming?"

"What I wanted to tell you . . ."

"Yes?"

There was a pause. I heard Sami's breath and had all possibilities right at the tip of my tongue, and all I said was, "I'm not prepared."

17

My boss was a small, pudgy man with a slight paunch and expensive suits made from light fabrics. He had asked me to come into his office for a serious talk. *Serious talk* were his words. I was afraid that meant he'd finally discovered just how superfluous my job was. When I entered he was standing behind his desk. With his right hand he pointed toward two armchairs in the corner. Above us hung a portrait of the chancellor.

I approached the armchairs and was about to sit down when he said, "That's my side."

He's going to fire me, I thought. I sat down in the other chair.

"Masha, there hasn't been that much to do lately.

That's partly because of the relatively calm political situation and partly because of severe budget cuts. And you've not been with us for very long."

I took a deep breath.

"I'm going to tell you something about hierarchies. You know that I'm your boss and therefore you should generally do as I say. I don't particularly feel like you have fully internalized that. You know, I have a boss, too, and my boss has a boss." He looked me in the eyes, checking whether his words reverberated in my soul. Then he pointed with the index finger of his right hand toward the portrait of Angela Merkel. "I'm not particularly fond of that boss. Do you think I want to be ruled over by a woman from East Germany? Do I care about East Germany? Don't make me laugh. But. I do as I'm told and I pay my taxes. Do you understand?"

I nodded.

"Next week our boss from Berlin is coming. As you know, our standing in Berlin is not exactly stellar. It's our Arab offices that get the most funding these days. The foundations that are active in Israel get less and less. That's just the general trend."

I nodded.

"I'll have to have several meetings with him. Present our work and our current projects to him. But he won't be alone. He's coming with company."

"His wife?"

"Not necessarily."

"Ah."

"The lady who is accompanying him is in the region for the first time and I want you to take care of her."

"Why me?"

"You're the same age. You are going to accompany her to Jerusalem."

"I don't speak any Hebrew."

"I've heard you speak. Why are you making such a big deal about it?"

"What does she want to do there in the first place?"

"Stroll through the market. Buy a few spices. What do I know? I'll have to talk with him and she needs a babysitter."

"I'm an interpreter."

"Precisely. Why not haggle in Arabic at the market?"

The next day I picked up my assignment. She was already waiting in front of the hotel, in a very short leather skirt and dark designer shades. Long hair with blond highlights. She'd recently gotten a manicure. I considered myself lucky that she didn't have a handbag dog. As a hello, she kissed my cheeks.

"I'm Maya. Thanks so much for coming along."

"My pleasure." I tried to smile just as fatuously as she did. "What would you like to see today?"

"I'd love to see the old town and then I want to see one of those settlements on the outskirts. I've read so much about them. So much injustice."

We strolled down Yaffo Street. Maya kept stopping to look at window displays or take a picture.

"Bringing a camera along is like having a toddler with you," she said coyly. Men on the street were constantly whistling at her. Even a few Orthodox Jews turned their heads, not as covertly as you might think.

Progress was slow through the old town. The narrow alleys were crammed with tourists, backpacks strapped to their chests, and believers from all across the denominational spectrum. Everyone in a fantasy uniform. The air was humid and stale. The merchants sat in front of their shops, yelling at the crowds: "Please, come in." "Do you want to see my shop?" "Natasha, Natasha, *idi syda.*" Maya smiled at each and every one of them.

We were surrounded by clothes, postcards, incense, glass pearls, cheap jewelry, henna colors, and pyramids of spices. Keffiyehs hung next to IDF shirts, sold by Arab and Jewish merchants in equal measure.

One even ran after us. He'd overheard us speaking German and asked us to write down the word *sale* in German for him. He wanted to lure us into his shop, but it wasn't necessary to lure Maya anywhere. I trudged behind the two.

In between keffiyehs and postcards, Maya told me and the merchants her life story. I abstained from translating. Born in Saarland. Her father was the mayor of her village (population: 200), her mother a home-maker. Home was crowded. Shortly after getting her trade school degree, she met an entrepreneur in a bar in Saarbrücken, much older than she. He took her along to Laos.

She tried on a dark blue scarf and the merchant held a mirror up to her. Lost in her own reflection, she continued: "I hardly remember my first husband. If I think about him at all, what comes to mind is the little black notebook with the blue lines that he always carried around with him. That's what he used to keep track of his bowel movements. Meticulously."

"Do you want to buy this scarf?" the merchant asked and I translated the question. She looked at me straight on, as if noticing my presence for the first time.

"I don't have any money on me." With her plas-tic nail, she tapped on the window. The shopkeeper understood the gesture and brought a different color. "In Laos I got used to the good things in life: spa treat-ments, massages, yoga, restaurants, delicacies, maids."

We continued our way through the old town. A woman lugging a shopping bag jostled me. Again and again we passed by heavily armed police patrols. I had to buy freshly squeezed orange juice for Maya. She drank it slowly as she rambled on. I had tried rattling off touristy folklore, to direct Maya's attention to an archaeological excavation or the Via Dolorosa, but she took every interruption of her monologue as an insult. When they returned to Germany, he immediately filed for divorce, without explanation. She got an apartment in Stuttgart and money, which she invested in diamond earrings, dresses, and a pearl necklace that had once belonged to a countess. And she got a tattoo. The sun had reached its highest point and I started heading toward the Austrian hospice. I could already imagine the taste of fresh lemonade on my tongue.

There, in the cool shade, she ordered the specialty of the house—apple strudel—and continued talking. She said the Jews were resting on the hard work of the Palestinians.

I remembered sitting in a waiting room with red leather chairs and an empty water cooler. My mother was with me. I was reading a magazine that was worn out from the many readers before me. All the crossword puzzles were already solved. In that magazine I'd spotted the article "The New Self-Confidence of the Jewish Community in Berlin." My mother was embarrassed. She was partial to quiet, unobtrusive Jews.

"Seeing that stuff, all that injustice on the evening news, really makes you hate the Jews. It's perfectly clear who the weak one is here, the victim," Maya said. She wiped the sweat off her forehead. "Look at all the things they've done to the Palestinians. They of all people should know better."

"German camps weren't exactly moral reformatories," I said.

She looked at me, suddenly a little insecure, laughed, and continued to gorge on the Austro-fascist strudel. One bite after the other disappeared into her mouth. Insatiable like a black hole. I called Sami and said that I would take the test, that I'd just quit my job.

18

I would let Tal know that I was sick of her games. That I'd had enough of her masturbatory wallowing in self-pity and that I was about to leave the city, and country, forever. Not brave enough to call her, I wrote an e-mail asking for a meeting in a small fish restaurant in Yaffo.

She didn't come. I'd sat alone at the table, the waitress waiting impatiently with the menu. Finally, I ordered a redfish that I didn't touch.

"Is something wrong with it?" the waitress asked, placing a carafe of water on the table.

"I'm not hungry," I answered.

"Then why'd you go out to eat?"

I paid, not leaving a tip, and went out to the street. Again and again, I checked my cellphone—no messages. I circled the taxi stand a couple of times. The drivers waited with motors running.

Riding through Tel Aviv in the back of a cab, loud mizrahi music blasting from the radio, the driver steering with one hand and tapping the beat with the other, I felt at home. It was a home long forgotten, a mosaic of landscape, temperature, music, smells, and the sea. I asked the driver to go along the beach and through the poorer southern Tel Aviv. That's when it occurred to me that the feeling of *home* was associated with places that reminded me of Baku.

The lock at the front door made suspicious noises. I was sure I'd been robbed. I unlocked the door and yelled, "Hello." To scare the burglars, I guess. It smelled funny, but the apartment was empty. On the kitchen table I discovered a limp bouquet and a note in Tal's handwriting: "Take care of the cats. Please." I found the cats in a carrier in my bedroom, their eyes glowing, hostile meows directed at me. A horrid smell was coming from the carrier.

"I need you," Tal said a week later. She sat huddled at my kitchen table, crying. Again and again, she sobbed loudly. Tal's eyes were bloodshot, her posture hunched, and her hair cut down to an inch.

"Where are my cats?" she asked as the crying ebbed away.

"In a shelter."

"You gave my cats away?"

"I didn't know if you'd come back."

"How can you be so cold?"

"You just ran away. Honestly I didn't think I'd ever see you again. Tal, what is it that you want?"

"Your help."

"You don't really mean that, do you?"

"We need a translator. Masha, you can't imagine what's going on there."

I didn't reply, because at that moment I understood that Tal wouldn't leave me. She would always be coming back, until she had sucked me dry completely. But there wasn't much left in me anyway.

"Just this one last time. Promise. If you still have feelings for me, then come with me." Tal placed her palms on my cheeks.

19

The summer air was hot and humid, like every day. By the time I made it down the five sets of stairs from my apartment to the street, I was soaked in sweat. In the supermarket, tourists were frantically looking for someone to translate the Hebrew product information. Others skeptically inspected the kashrut confirmation on the packaging. I bought coffee and milk, then crossed the street toward the fast-food restaurants.

The Indian food sat in two small boxes. Elias wasn't hungry. He lay on the couch apathetically, covered by a light blanket, flipping through channels. I sat down next to him and snuggled up. I wanted to feel his warmth, kiss him and stroke him, but he didn't move, wouldn't grant me even the slightest tenderness. Rigor mortis had already set in.

part four

1

None of the incoming cars was stopped at the check-point. All the energy went into inspecting the cars that went the other way, into Israel. Tal's thin hands clasped the steering wheel, white knuckles protruding. I hadn't asked where we were going, didn't want to know. In the back were three boys, all vegans, squirming nervously in their seats.

"Do you have your passport?" Tal asked and shot me an irritated glance. She wore a prim dress that covered her shoulders and knees. It was the color of an Afghan burka. We passed the checkpoint and then a construction site, where an entire block of luxury condos was being erected.

"What would happen if I was to discover in Ramallah that I didn't have my passport on me? Do you think they wouldn't let me back into Israel?"

"This is not your average Sunday outing," Tal said.

"Looks like Sunday to me."

We didn't speak for the rest of the way.

Tal left the car in the city center, right next to the grave of a late Fatah fighter. The grave was decorated with flowers, like a roadside memorial for someone who had died in a car accident. Above the grave was a huge billboard displaying a picture of the deceased, a lanky man in a wool pullover holding a machine gun. The barrel of the gun was pointed directly at his own grave. As if we were shooting himself until eternity. On the side of the road were expensive SUVs with stickers bearing the logos of international aid organizations.

The vegans were standing next to the car, a little uncertain. I speculated that they were embarrassed to be overheard speaking Hebrew—which would have been somewhat inappropriate in the middle of Ramallah—but nobody wanted to be the first to break into English. None of them spoke Arabic, which was why they now stuck to their embarrassed silence. I could've done them the favor of saying something and thereby establishing English as the language of choice, but I didn't.

Tal went ahead. Her steps were long and energetic—
we had trouble keeping up. It was a rainy Friday morning and the city center was deserted. I assumed that
most men were at the mosque and women at home. I
counted the doorbell signs of international NGOs, UN
schools, and parking lots supported by the European
Union. A parade of the new colonialism.

Tal took to it like a duck to water. No sign of her
nervousness.

"Here." Tal pointed at a house.

I said hello into the intercom, the heavy iron gate
opened, and a petite woman approached us. Her face
was powdery and her eyes black-rimmed.

Salam had a firm handshake and the habit of looking whomever she was talking to directly in the eyes.
She told us to take a seat in her living room and disappeared into the kitchen.

The curtains were closed and the floor was covered
in soft wool rugs. It was a large room and as far as I
could discern in the dim light, reproductions of French
impressionists and large oil paintings hung on the wall.
Judging by the quality of the latter, they might have
been painted by one of the inhabitants. A Marianne,
gripping a Palestinian flag, with chastely covered, if
remarkably large, breasts. A crying child with blood
smeared on its head, and an old, bent man in a loamy,
dark prison cell, eyes cast longingly at a small window

above. The painter had gotten the perspective wrong, but at least now the window looked out straight onto the dome of the rock. Every last remaining bit of free wall space was taken up by bookshelves.

On the table in front of us was a bowl of fruit—peaches, nectarines, and mangos. Other bowls held pieces of watermelon, dried fruits, and nuts. Salam came back with fresh juice, Turkish coffee, and sweet pastries. I complimented her on the pastries. She complimented me on my Arabic and asked about my Lebanese dialect.

Tal absentmindedly drew circles on the tablecloth. I said that I'd learned Arabic from my fiancé, who had been born in Beirut. I wasn't quite sure why I lied to her, but it felt good to talk about Sami. Salam switched to English and that brought the small talk to a close.

Before getting down to business, everyone told their story, probably a pedagogical technique. Tal sat at the end of the sofa and slowly tore a paper napkin into pieces. Every muscle in her body was tense. When it was her turn all she said was: "Tal. We've been in touch."

Salam nodded at her briefly and said, "I'm from a traumatized family. My father is a member of the Palestine Communist Party and has spent ten years in Israeli prisons. I always dreamed of becoming a doctor. After graduating, I got a scholarship to go to Prague, to study genetics."

Salam took a break and topped off everyone's coffee. Then she looked at me strangely and asked, "Are you OK?"

"Yes," I replied.

Tal's dress was light blue. Not dark blue, not ultramarine, not azure, not gray blue. Light blue. She didn't even look at me. I rummaged through my bag for some benzodiazepine pills, but I couldn't find any.

"When I arrived in Prague, I knew nothing. I'd never even set foot in a lab before. They were forbidden in Palestine. Israel was afraid schoolkids would learn how to build bombs instead of studying biology." Tal winced at the word *bomb*. Maybe she was thinking of her aunt and uncle.

"I was like a Bedouin seeing a city for the first time. I had to learn everything, even how to hold the equipment. When I finally caught up with the other students, the Soviet Union collapsed. As the others were celebrating, I was packing my suitcase. My stipend was through the Communist Party, which had collapsed along with the Soviet Union. I couldn't afford the tuition. I didn't have rich parents, or a rich husband. In Palestine, I enrolled to study diplomacy."

"Why diplomacy of all things?" Yoni asked. He was one of the two guys who had come.

"Why not? There were still no labs so I couldn't continue my studies, and diplomacy seemed like a good idea at the time."

"Not anymore?"

"Not as long as it contributes to normalization," said Tal and she looked Salam directly in the eyes. Salam nodded and smiled. They understood each other.

I felt nothing for her anymore. Neither hate nor love, not even affection.

2

Small groups of men and boys passed me in the opposite direction. Suits, dark mustaches. Most shops were still closed, the sky was gray and I had goose bumps from the cold. I looked down, trying to avoid the long puddles. I was searching for a cafe where a woman by herself wouldn't get into trouble. It had gotten dark and I knew that what I was doing was pure insanity anyway.

"I'm Ismael."

He introduced himself in English and I answered in Arabic. Ismael respectfully held out his hand for me to shake. He had a surprisingly limp handshake for a man of his height. He seemed very young.

Once I'd realized that my feelings for Tal had vanished, I'd excused myself, saying I had to go to the bathroom. Then I climbed through the window and ran into the street. Now I was sitting by myself in the center of Ramallah. Surrounded by a dozen men in suits. But Ismael was the only one who spoke to me.

"Where are you from?"

"Germany."

"Really?"

"Yes."

He sat down next to me.

"Where did you learn Arabic? From a man?" he asked.

"Yes."

"Are you married?"

I nodded.

Ismael sighed. "Me, too. Difficult. You don't look like a German at all."

"How do Germans look?"

"I don't know."

"And Russians?" I asked him. "How do they look?"

He shrugged and said, "Like people who love birch trees."

"Americans?"

"Look around you. Palestine is full of them."

"And Palestinians?"

"Like people who are used to waiting a long time."

I laughed and Ismael grinned, pleased. Leaning back, he lit a cigarette.

"You are cold," he said.

"No."

"You are. I can see it. Take my jacket."

"No."

Ismael took off his jacket and placed it on the table. I shook my head and the jacket remained where it was. Now we were both cold.

"What are you doing here?"

I smiled and shrugged.

"Are you waiting for someone?"

I shook my head no.

"Do you work here? Are you part of an international organization? Or did you marry a rich Arab?"

Ismael ran his fingers through his hair, slowly and with both hands, his brows furrowed. He had the same gestures as Elisha and a similar voice.

"What do you do?" I asked.

"Mostly . . . I get myself into trouble." He laughed at his own joke. "I'm a photographer."

I grinned. It all matched up.

"You're smiling for no reason. I'm not an artist. I'm a wedding photographer."

"Do you enjoy it?"

"Such a question can only come from a German. It pays the bills, that's what matters most. Well, almost.

The middle class in Palestine is pretending to be American high society. Which is good for me, since I'm making money off of that. Tomorrow I'll take pictures of a wedding here, in a hotel in Ramallah, and the day after tomorrow I'm going to Jenin."

"I was born in Azerbaijan," I said.

"That's far away."

"Not that far."

"That's a Muslim country, isn't it? Are you a Muslim?" he asked.

"No."

"Christian?"

I shook my head. Ismael laughed and said, "Great! Then you're a member of my denomination."

"What is your denomination?"

"Rastafarian. Can I get you anything to drink?"

"No thanks."

Ismael came back with two cups of Turkish coffee. He set one down in front of me, his eyes meeting mine.

"Would you do me a favor?" he asked.

"What is it?"

"Put on the jacket. You're shivering. And seriously, what are you doing here?"

"Running away." The words slipped out.

"From your husband? Did you cheat on him?"

I didn't answer. Ismael ran both his hands through his hair again.

"Your husband is Arab, right?"

I nodded.

"Oh, man. That'll end badly, I'm telling you."

I shook my head and suddenly realized that a tear was running down my face. I couldn't believe that I was crying over my own lies. I had a German passport, a well-paid job, and an apartment in Tel Aviv. I was free. Instead, I was sitting by myself in a cafe in Ramallah, crying and making up stories for a complete stranger. Just because he resembled Elisha. I felt a pain in my chest, like a needle piercing my lung. Everything went black. I shivered, struggling to remain conscious.

"Do you have anybody you can stay with?" Ismael's words reverberated, muffled in my head. He put his jacket around my shoulders. I wanted to calm down, swallowed deep breaths, massaged my temples. I tried to look at him, to smile, but the pain grew worse, insistently clawing deeper into my stomach, my lungs, my heart, until my whole body was one black mass of pain.

I slowly breathed in and out—the pain was gone.

It was only then that I opened my eyes. I realized with some relief that I wasn't in a hospital. I was lying on a sofa in a small, dark room. Ismael sat on the other end of the sofa, making sure that my legs were up. When he saw that I had come to again, he immediately took his hands off of me.

"Where am I?"

"In the cafe's office," Ismael whispered. "Are you feeling better?"

"Yes. Thank you."

I got up.

"Where are you going?"

"To settle the bill."

"I guess you haven't lost your sense of humor."

"I'm fine," I said as I swayed.

Ismael regarded me seriously.

"And where are you going, anyway?"

I raised my shoulders and let them slump again. "I don't know."

"You can stay with me. We can figure it out from there."

I nodded. "Thanks."

"I'll get the car, then I'll come and pick you up. Do you have any luggage?"

I shook my head. Ismael left the room, then called out from the stairway: "Brave of you to marry an Arab."

When I woke up it was midnight. I turned on the light. On the nightstand was a plastic bag, the color-ful logo of a drugstore printed on the side. In it I found a toothbrush, toothpaste, a hairbrush, and skin toner. Ismael had thought of everything. I got up and went to the window, pulling back the curtain ever so slightly, like a voyeur. It looked out onto a parking lot. Nine rows of parked cars, illuminated by powerful neon lights and a guard booth with a TV flickering inside.

Ismael had insisted that I sleep in his double bed. "No discussion," he had said and pulled the door shut behind him. He'd huddled up in the bathtub, a blanket between him and the cold enamel, the pillow in his lap. I went to check on him a couple of times during the night. Saw him turning in his sleep, trying to adapt his body to the bathtub's contours. In the early morning he lay stretched out on the tiles, between the sink and the toilet, quietly snoring.

That morning, he ordered room service, hung his camera over his shoulder, and left me alone with the food. I slept until noon, got up, took a long shower, and left.

The city center was pure chaos. Lurid colors and crowds of people filling every inch between honking cars, open workshops, cafes, veiled mothers with small, screaming children, Bedouins, Osama's Pizzeria, and bakeries that made pita bread on round metal plates. It was only when I stepped out on the street and noticed the reactions around me that I became aware that I was walking around half naked by Arab standards.

From one instant to the next, I lost my strength. I barely managed to make my way to an inner courtyard. Once there, I crouched down next to two overflowing trash cans, the smell of sewage in the air. For a moment, I was sure I couldn't bear it any longer. I thought I might scream. Then the intensity of the pain slowly ebbed off, until I could stand again and go.

"There are two options." I said to Ismael when I entered the hotel room. He was standing next to the window, in an undershirt and boxer shorts. Tall and sinewy. He'd just gotten out of the shower and his scent was a mix of musky aftershave and flowery shower gel. A cigarette hung from the corner of his mouth. He quickly reached for his pants that lay on the bed and put them on.

"So, there are only two options," I started again. "Either I wear this dress and get stoned as a harlot, or I put on something longer. But then I look like a Jewish settler and I'll still get stoned."

Ismael stubbed out his cigarette in the ashtray, grinning. "I hope you'll go with the first option."

I sighed. "I knew you'd say that."

"It's not what you think. But I suspect it would be easier to save your life this way."

I put my shopping bag down on the bed.

"What's that?" he asked.

"Our picnic."

"On the bed?"

I nodded.

"We don't have any plates."

"I bought some. Cutlery, too."

Ismael flung the pillows off the bed and sat down. He crossed his legs and watched me as I emptied my bag: fresh bread, olives, hummus, falafel, cheese and pastrami from a European deli, fruit, and Malabi.

We sat across from each other, eating in silence. I spotted a long scar on Ismael's forearm that looked like it had come from a burn.

"Where'd you get that?"

He shrugged: "A bullet."

"Israeli?"

"I didn't ask about the manufacturer." He smiled, lowering his shoulders again. "Maybe a German one, who knows? They call it development aid here."

There were many more scars on his arms and on his chin, too. I didn't dare ask how he got those. Ismael lit a joint and handed it to me. That night he slept in the bathroom again.

It took me a long time to fall asleep. I tossed from one side to the next. Then I dreamed of Elisha. He was wearing his hospital gown, his mouth contorted in pain. He was suffering. I wanted to touch him but he wouldn't let me, said that I had let him die.

3

We bounced in our seats as the car rumbled in and out of potholes. "We should've taken the donkey," Ismael said and put in an old cassette tape. Bob Dylan. Ismael drummed the rhythm on the steering wheel. Barely one song in we were stopped by a road block. Two guys in bulletproof vests pointed the barrels of their guns at us. The Palestinian policemen were even younger than the Israeli soldiers, sixteen years old at most. We handed our passports to them through the windows before they ordered us out. They kept us in sight. Ismael asked one of the two whether he liked belly dancing. Once they finally dourly handed us back our documents, we continued on our way. From then on, we only listened to Fairuz.

We stopped in a small village and sat down in a restaurant with green plastic chairs that served shawarma.
Once again I was the only woman in the room.

The wall across from the restaurant was full of graf-
fiti. Somebody had written in green *Allahu Akbar,*
and another one "Sister, fear Allah—don't take off
your hijab." Next to that in unsteady handwriting,
"Fuck Israel" and "Fuck PA, Fuck Hamas." Farther
down someone had added with a Sharpie, "Fuck me,
if you want."

Ismael followed my gaze and pointed toward the
house in front of us. "Do you see the water tanks on
the houses?"

I nodded.

"Israel fills them twice a week. And that's it. If you
use up the water too quickly, that's your problem. No
one will help you." Ismael looked at me. "I hope that's
not too much for you to take in?"

"We didn't have water either."

"What?"

"In Baku we had a maximum of one hour of water
per day, and not even regularly. In that hour you'd fill
everything with water: tanks, tubs, bottles."

"OK, you win."

A swastika was etched into our table. I traced the
lines with my fingers.

"So I was a part of Hamas," Ismael said all of a sudden. "So what?"

I lifted my head. Our eyes met. I downed my glass of water and Ismael refilled it.

"But they didn't help me either. You want to know how it all started?" Ismael didn't wait for my answer. "Soccer. I played soccer. Two times a week. First we ran after the ball, then we ran after God. Religious school was introduced after the training. And suddenly I had a beard—it grows a lot faster with Arabs than you're probably used to with European men. On the other hand, you're from Azerbaijan. That's more like here. I was wearing a long white robe and a hood." He turned to me and laughed. "Fooled you! I never wore a robe, but I was devout. Always averted my eyes when there was a woman on TV. And my mother. We fought a lot. Now I regret it, but then I looked down on her because she didn't wear a hijab."

"I'm Jewish."

Ismael fell silent. Shaking his head, he ran a hand through his hair. He fished a pack of dented Marlboros from his pocket, lit a cigarette, smoked it, threw it onto the ground, and crushed it with his boot.

"At least that's not contagious. Let's go."

Ismael insisted on paying, despite my protests.

———

As we drove, I looked out the window at the passing landscape. Arab villages, Israeli settlements, mountains. We listened to music. Mashrou' Leila. I got drunk on the music and the beauty of the scenery and I thought that the first Zionists to come to Palestine when the British Mandate had been in place must have been drunk on the landscape, too. Ismael lit a cigarette. Israel or Palestine, I didn't care. I'd had enough.

"Are you Israeli?" he asked.

"I don't even speak Hebrew."

"I do. I've worked construction in Tel Aviv. Before the wall. Why didn't you emigrate to Israel?"

"I wanted to, but my parents were against it."

He abruptly turned toward me: "Are you fucking with me?"

"When did you leave Hamas?" I asked.

"After only half a year. There were long discussions. They even came to my house with presents once. Like the three kings, in case you know your Bible. They wanted to convince my parents, but my parents were Communists. Nothing doing. A friend who had stayed with Hamas declared a fatwa against me via Facebook. That's when I knew I'd made the right decision."

Ismael lit another cigarette.

"My parents were Communists, too," I said.

"You know, when I was a kid, I always had to recite the Communist Manifesto as a punishment," Ismael said and laughed.

"Shit."

"Exactly. But now my father's into religion. Prays five times a day and is on the lookout for a second wife. My mother is still a Communist. She even ran in the last election. There were posters with her name and face all over the city. A great honor. My father told everyone he wouldn't vote for her. And he didn't."

"Did she win?"

"Who's going to vote for you if not even your husband will?"

We were silent for a while.

"You know, I went to Germany once. Good country, but they won't let you smoke anywhere. I missed Palestine. As soon as I got back I lit a cigarette. I hadn't even left the bus."

Ismael was steering with only one hand. In the other he held a cigarette.

"But one thing I still don't get," he said. "Why did your father marry a Jew?"

"He just fell in love."

Ismael grinned at me for a moment too long.

"What do you believe in?" he asked.

"Nothing."

"God?"

"No."

"Culture?"

"Nope."

"Nation?"

"You know, when I was a kid everyone kept a packed suitcase. Precautionary measure. With us, it was my grandfather's old briefcase. In it there was fresh underwear, family pictures, silver spoons, and gold crowns—the capital they were able to accumulate in a Communist regime. The Armenians had already been driven out of the city. Many were executed. My grandma, who had witnessed the Shoah . . ."

"OK, I got the hint!"

4

By the time we passed the sign that said it was three miles to Jenin, we were already in the city.

"This area was the hardest hit during the second intifada," Ismael said. "In 2002, the Israeli army invaded the refugee camp."

"Following an attack by Hamas," I pointed out.

"Yes, following an attack by Hamas. Multiple attacks even. Listen, I don't want to sugarcoat or sanctify anything. I just want to tell you how it was."

"Sorry."

"So, do you want me to continue?"

"Yeah, of course."

"For days, there were street battles. Until they came with bulldozers. They plowed through everything, even the houses with people in them. In the end, we couldn't tell what was a dead body and what was an animal cadaver. When they finally left, everything was silent. Even the air. Especially the air. It had stopped circulating. The smell of drying blood everywhere. All I smelled was the scent of decay, and even though I'd gotten through it with only a flesh wound, I felt dead. I was certain I would die before too long. I had taken on that scent."

The refugee camp was a village with narrow streets. I hadn't noticed the transition between the city and the camp. We stopped in front of a whitewashed house and the parking brake clicked into place.

"We can't kiss or hug," Ismael said, despite the fact that—up to this point—we hadn't even touched. Not even an accidental brushing of clothes. The driver's door opened and slammed shut. I took a deep breath, then exited the car.

"By the way, my cousin's getting married," he said.

"Why didn't you tell me?"

"Because then you might not have come. I should also mention that I have three sisters and two brothers, not to mention dozens of cousins, aunts, uncles, and nephews."

And as soon as we neared the house, twelve women came out, smothering Ismael in kisses and hugs. He introduced a small, delicate woman to me as his mother. Then he disappeared in the yard and I was interrogated. Some women wore a hijab, others didn't. I said that I was an international peace activist, which settled the matter: this kind of woman was not uncommon in Palestine and nobody asked about my stance on Ismael.

One of Ismael's sisters led me up a steep spiraling staircase. I had to hold on to the handrail. Haifa was the youngest sister. She had curious dark brown eyes and full lips. Her shiny dark hair fell over her shoulders, reaching down to her waist. Haifa sat me down on her bed and started to give me a makeover. She straightened my hair, trimmed my eyebrows with a piece of thread, applied makeup and perfume. The dress she lent me was light blue.

"You're beautiful," Haifa said as we both regarded her work in the mirror. "But when we meet the others, you probably shouldn't mention that you're a peace activist."

"Why not?" I asked.

Embarrassed, she looked to the floor. "Well, we're kind of fed up with peace. We want rights and a state. The peace process is a failure and we don't want normalization."

"But I already told everyone."

"Doesn't matter, just don't repeat it. And, besides . . ." Here she paused, averted her eyes.

"Yes?"

"Ismael has already had enough trouble lately," she said in a firm voice.

I didn't inquire further, because it wasn't any of my business and because I was sure she'd tell me anyway. But to my surprise, her expression turned to anger and she yelled, "I don't understand you people! You come here as volunteers and think that you can do what you want because you're so nice. So awfully nice. You don't give a shit about us. Our role is simply to suffer and install your air conditioners."

I stared at her. Haifa nodded and continued: "But oh well. He brought you here, now you're our guest. I'm sorry. It's just that normalization is the wrong way. We have to strengthen the resistance against the occupation and not play into its hands. You Germans, you're so naive." Somehow her explanation rang false. I could tell she wasn't speaking her mind, but couldn't quite place the dissonance.

Haifa took me by the hand and led me into the living room to the other women. The men were outside in the garden celebrating.

The bride was made up like a doll and surrounded by women. Whoever wasn't dancing was clapping along. The music was loud and the air full of heavy scents.

Everyone had taken off their coats and hijabs. I caught a glimpse of myself in the mirror. Blue dress. The music was deafening and outside it was still day.

I went out onto the street that smelled of sewage. Somewhere a chicken squawked. I walked through the narrow alleys. On the walls hung posters of prisoners doing time in Israeli prisons and of suicide bombers with the specifics of their date of death. Between them hung ads. I kept noticing swastikas everywhere I went. I thought of the Caspian Sea, of the pleasure boats and Rostropovich. I wanted to go home. Back to my mother. Wanted her to protect me. Back to Elisha, to clasp his shirt, breathe in his smell, see his face clearly in front of me again. I had goose bumps that refused to go away and a rising sickness inside me. I tried to rest, leaned against a wall to gather energy. My nose bled. A small boy passed me on his bike. He rung the bell and yelled something, but his voice was distorted and I didn't understand. After a while he gave up and biked on. I noticed that I was standing next to a butcher shop. Entire cadavers hung in the shop window, upside down on a silver hook. Next door was Café Baghdad. In their window hung a profile shot of Saddam Hussein. I walked toward it, reaching out for it, pressing my hand against the cold window.

"Saddam, you again," I said. "Do you remember the name of the redheaded boy? The one from the park?"

No answer. Saddam was dead. Elisha was dead. Everything was dead. The Days of Sacrifice. My father hung blankets over our windows because the soldiers shot like moths fly: always into the light. An unnatural silence hung over the city. Dark clouds covered the sky, as if to muffle every sound. My father wore his black coat. A duffel bag hung over his shoulder. My mother had quickly packed my things: thick wool socks, dresses, pullovers. She quietly cried as she did so. Buttoning my coat, she looked at me, then she removed my necklace with the Star of David, which I had worn since I was three. I protested but she said that this wasn't the time for it. Go. My father pulled me after him. There were hardly any people on the street. In front of some houses lay smashed furniture, slit mattresses, random pieces of clothing. Windows were shattered, broken glass littered the cobblestones, mingling with pieces of random family photos.

"Hurry up," my father said.

Above us, screams, a cacophony of yelling and a drawn-out female voice. The sound of the body hitting the asphalt. The blue of her dress. The puddle of blood. My father tried shutting my eyes. I freed myself. Ran to her. Her blood stained my shoes crimson red. My father didn't want to leave me alone. Grandmother yelled at my father. Go. Go back to your wife. Then she tried to calm me down. She wrapped me in a blanket and had me lie down on her bed. My nose started bleeding. Somebody knocked on the door, but grandmother wouldn't open it.

"Aunt Anna, Aunt Anna. Open the door," somebody yelled from the other side. "It's me, Abbas, your former student from third grade."

Grandmother didn't move.

"Open the door. I'm with the National Front."

My grandmother mumbled a Yiddish curse and then backed it up with a Russian one. Then she unlocked the door. A man entered the hallway. His fur cap was pulled down low, his hands were red from the cold and a machine gun hung from his shoulder.

"Aunt Anna, you are hiding Armenians. Someone reported you."

"Are you crazy?" she asked and stood there, hands on her hips.

I came into the hall. My dress was smeared with blood, which was still running from my nose. The man looked at me, startled. He asked my grandmother, "What's wrong with her?"

"She was outside, that's what's wrong with her. What are you guys doing?" she yelled.

He looked from me to my grandmother, didn't say a word, but couldn't quite bring himself to leave, either.

He took off his hat. Pearls of sweat gathered on his upper lip.

"I'll have to search the apartment," he mumbled.

"After you." Grandmother gestured, inviting him in. He nodded and went back out to the stairway. My grandmother locked the door behind him. She sank to the floor. *Everything repeats itself,* she muttered. *Everything repeats itself. Everything repeats itself.*

I continued my way through the narrow streets. I passed by a barricade. In front of it was a fire surrounded by five men speaking Azeri and warming their hands. A tank approached us, flattening a parked car in its path. From a window above, someone threw a Molotov cocktail. It descended like a falling star, leaving a trail in its wake. At the time, I had been fascinated by the image. I was looking for Ismael's car, but I couldn't find it. Walked in circles until I couldn't breathe anymore, then tried to get out. Artemis and Shushanik had been the names of the daughters of Grandmother's friend. Her name had been Gajane. Suddenly the tank came to a halt, its prow turned, and the cannon swiveled to aim at the window where the attack had come from. A shattering blast left a hole in the neighboring house. Inside you could see a kitchen table and flowery tapestry. As I brushed a strand of hair from my face, the blood smeared across my cheek.

Sami answered on the first ring. I heard a woman laughing in the background and Sami asked the person who was laughing to please be quiet.

"Come and get me, please," I said.

"Where are you?"

I looked around, but didn't know anymore where I was. I had left the camp and now was standing more or less in a field. I was surrounded by olive trees, each looking exactly like the other. On the horizon I saw the bright red roofs of a settlement.

"Don't be silly, tell me immediately where you are."

I tried to sound normal: "I don't know."

"Are you in Tel Aviv?"

"Palestine. I'm standing in the middle of a field. The sun is setting."

"I'll take the next flight. I'll be there tomorrow morning."

"Sami, I'm losing blood."

Elisha hands me a tissue. I put it to my nose and lean my head back. "You have to hold up your head. Otherwise the bleeding won't stop."

"Higher," Elisha says. "Yes, exactly like that."

I take his arm, and for a while we walk side by side. The sun has almost set, but it's still light out.

Acknowledgments

My sincere thanks go to Lala Bashi, Alexej Grjasnow, Norbert Gstrein, Sophie Knigge, Petra Maria Kraxner, and Julia Kreuzer, without whom I would never have begun, let alone finished, this book; and to Mustafa Staiti, Farnoush Noori, and Lina Muzur, as well as my parents, Julija Winnikova and Oleg Grjasnow.

Many thanks also to the Rosa Luxemburg Foundation and the Simon Literary Agency.

OLGA GRJASNOWA was born in 1984 in Baku, Azerbaijan, grew up in the Caucasus, and has spent extended periods in Poland, Russia, and Israel. She moved to Germany at the age of twelve and is a graduate of the German Institute for Literature/Creative Writing in Leipzig. *All Russians Love Birch Trees,* for which she received a research grant from the Robert Bosch Foundation, has won the Kühne Prize, the Anna Seghers Prize, and was long-listed for the German Book Prize in 2012.

EVA BACON studied German and English Literature at the Ludwig Maximilians University of Munich and has worked as an international literary scout. This is her first translation of a novel. She lives in Brooklyn, New York.